I0717590

The Rock Star and the Billionaire

DEMELZA CARLTON

Book 4 in the Romance Island Resort series

Copyright © 2016 Demelza Carlton

Lost Plot Press

ISBN-13: 978-1-925799-08-8

ISBN-10: 1-925799-08-5

DEDICATION

This book is for all my awesome readers. Yes, you.
You buy, read, love and review my books…and let me
know how much you love them.
That's something not even billionaires can buy.
You rock star, you.

ONE

Only the sky cried at Morrigan Vasse's funeral. Every mourner's eyes were dry beneath the canopy of black umbrellas – including those of Morrigan's only daughter and heiress, Gaia Vasse. It wasn't that she didn't care. Gaia's emotionless exterior hid a storm of feelings that ranged from desolation at her loss to triumph at the chance to prove herself, with a strong strand of anger at her mother for dying without warning. But if there was one thing Gaia's mother had taught her, it was never to share her thoughts with her inferiors. And these people in their cheap black clothes were definitely her inferiors. They all owed Morrigan their livelihood. At least, they had until a heart attack had conquered the powerful mining magnate. Now, they and the whole of Vasse Prospecting belonged to Gaia.

"Would Miss Vasse like to say a few words?"

Gaia met the eyes of the celebrant. This was not on the carefully laid out order of service she'd paid him for. A glance at the mourners made her reconsider the refusal on the tip of her tongue, for the air of expectancy was thicker than the drizzle falling from the sky. Morrigan had always insisted on taking every opportunity to address her people, as she'd called her employees, if only to remind them that she was in charge. And Gaia was Morrigan's daughter, trained from her earliest days to take over her mother's responsibilities. She'd been pushed into public speaking in preschool, learned the principles of business before she'd finished primary school. All preparation for the life she'd live. Starting today.

Clearing her throat, Gaia waited for silence to fall before she clearly enunciated, "Vale, Mother." With practiced ease, she tossed the white lilium she'd clutched in her gloved fingers. It landed at the head of the coffin, over where Gaia imagined Morrigan's traitorous heart now lay, silenced forever.

The celebrant waited for a moment, as if he expected her to say more, but at Gaia's sharp nod, he continued the service to its merciful end. The lesser mourners tossed their flowers with less precision than Gaia, until the coffin was buried in them.

Gaia suppressed a snort. Her mother had always despised cut flowers. She'd likened them to tortured slaves. First, they were cut and separated from their parent plant, then kept alive by artificial means in water while being imprisoned in freezing cold, airless refrigerators until they were displayed in all their dying glory on some table, to be admired as they perished. That hadn't stopped Morrigan from filling her house and office with the things – quite the opposite. What most people didn't know was that Morrigan had enjoyed arranging the displays with her own hands. It was one of her few hobbies, to create works of floral art in the Japanese ikebana style. When people frustrated her, Morrigan had resorted to torturing flowers and bending them to her implacable will.

She wouldn't push her frustrations on flowers like her mother had, bottling it all up until her heart perished from the stress. No, Gaia intended to do business differently, by bending people to her will. She might be her mother's daughter, but she was not her mother, as the departing mourners would soon learn.

In her distraction, she found herself alone by her mother's graveside. No, not quite alone – one man stood on the other side of the coffin, his face obscured by his low-held umbrella. For a moment, Gaia's heart leaped as she wondered if it was her father, but the man folded his umbrella under his arm and she recognised her mother's managing director, James Stewart. The only man her mother had ever listened to, or so she said. Gaia thought she'd only listened to him long enough to formulate an argument to do the complete opposite of whatever he'd advised.

Did he intend to antagonise her here, of all places? At her mother's damn funeral?

Stewart met her glare with irritating calm. He strode around the hole that held her mother's boxed body and offered Gaia his hand. "Miss Vasse, my condolences for your loss."

She accepted the handshake out of politeness, more than anything else. Stewart was older than her mother. Older than she had been when she died, Gaia reminded herself. It would take her a long time to get used to the fact that she was gone.

He coughed. "May I ask when you'll feel ready to take up the reins of Vasse Prospecting?" When she didn't immediately reply, he continued, "Of course, I understand that your mother's death was quite a shock to you, as it was to us all, so I wouldn't want to intrude on your grief. If you'll tell me when you plan on coming into the office, I can arrange – "

"Tomorrow," Gaia interrupted. "You'll get your new chairman tomorrow." She hid her smile at the shock on his face.

Stewart closed his mouth, then cleared his throat again. "If you're sure you're ready, Miss Vasse. There's the urgent matter of Lorikeet Island and we need a decision – "

"Tomorrow, Stewart. It can wait until tomorrow." Now she let her face twist into a grim smile. "I buried my mother today. She's not even cold in her grave. A bit of respect, please."

"Of course." He still looked like he wanted to argue.

Before he could decide that Lorikeet Island needed her attention more than common courtesy would allow, Gaia set off toward her car. She had a wake to attend, wearing a false smile as she accepted the condolences of all the mourners who'd been at the cemetery and now expected a free feed.

Freeloaders at funerals. If she had any say in it, there'd be none at hers. If people wanted to eat and drink themselves stupid when she died, they could pay for it out of their own pockets. She ground the accelerator under her custom-made black shoe, and her car left a satisfying spray of gravel in its wake.

TWO

Gaia eyed the graduation photo on her mother's – now her – desk. Her in the black gown and cap all MBA graduates wore; Mother in the gown and floppy hat of her latest in a string of honorary doctorates. If she needed a family photo in here to make her look more like her staff, then it wasn't a bad choice. It was a reminder of whose daughter she was; as well as evidence that she was qualified by more than money to sit in the chairman's seat. Vasse Prospecting was her domain now.

"Miss Vasse? Have you had a chance to look over the latest report about Lorikeet Island? I left it on your desk last night." Stewart strode smoothly into the office, as if he owned the place. Not even a knock.

Gaia's gaze settled on him. "No. I'll call you when I'm ready to discuss it."

"Miss Vasse, if you'll allow me to brief you, we can – "

"No, I won't, and no, we can't." She took a deep breath, then blew it out her nose. She wished she could breathe flame to show the arrogant managing director her fury. "This is my company, Stewart. I'll act when I'm ready."

He backed up. "You should know that the seawall, which was weakened in the last cyclone, broke two days ago. While you were waiting to act. Now, Lorikeet Island mine is completely flooded. You have no choice but to close it down." Gaia caught a glimpse of his triumphant smile before he turned and marched out of her office.

Insufferable man. He'd been in charge when the mine flooded, which made it his fault, not hers. It couldn't be as bad as he said.

But that didn't make it any less her problem now. An incompetent managing director meant more work for her.

Sighing, she sent her assistant to get her some tea while she opened the file on Lorikeet Island.

THREE

The thick file took her most of the morning. She'd toyed with the idea of calling in Stewart and making him stand before her desk like a schoolboy delivering a book report while he briefed her, but she needed to understand Lorikeet Island for herself. She knew its history, after all. Who didn't?

Other investors had made their fortune in mining Western Australia's wealth. All the rest of them had focussed on the mainland. But Stanley Vasse, fresh out of the army from his service in World War II, had other ideas. He'd been stationed at secret bases in Western Australia's remote north, only accessible by boat and plane, and he'd seen enough of the islands to know the wealth they held. Not gold, but red gold — iron ore, which gave the pindan dust up there its bloody hue. And the world needed iron, what with all that would need to be rebuilt once the war was over.

So when the war ended, he fought for his islands. It took six long years of sampling and testing and mapping before he staked his claim on Lorikeet Island, one of the highest quality reefs of iron ore in the world. As he demonstrated when his mine crews started to dig. They mined the cliffs, and when those were gone, he brought in geologists and oceanographers to map the sea bed, before he reclaimed that, too. And the red mud ran like blood, dripping dollars into the Vasse family coffers until her grandfather could afford other islands and other mines, diamonds and coal and uranium, if the government would ever get their arses into gear and let them dig up the damn radioactive stuff. Vasse Prospecting had owned the mining leases on an untouched deposit of uranium for more than sixty years, but hadn't been allowed to raise a single tonne of yellowcake. That would soon change, though. Under Gaia's management, Vasse Uranium had secured the necessary approvals to start mining. By this time next year, her flagship project would be turning a profit. She'd succeeded where her mother and her grandfather had failed. Vasse luck was on the rise once more with her at the helm, and there was nothing she wouldn't do to ensure it continued.

Mother had once told her that she'd sell everything else she owned – mines, properties, all their other investments – but as long as they owned Lorikeet Island, their fortunes were assured. The seabed around the island held enough iron ore to keep the mine open for another century at least. More if it extended to the other nearby islands.

So there was no way she'd ever approve Stewart's

planned shutdown of Lorikeet Island mine. No matter how many pictures he'd included in his report, showing the lagoon where the seawall had until recently kept out the ocean, it wasn't enough to make her change her mind. They would rebuild, as they always had, and the mine would reopen as soon as possible.

A tentative knock at the door.

Gaia raised her head, but Harrison, her mother's assistant, kept his eyes lowered. "Your tea, Miss Vasse."

"Is it Earl Grey this time?" she demanded.

He reddened. "Yes, ma'am." He set the offering on her desk and whisked away the cold cup from her previous one. She'd lost count of how much she'd drunk this morning, and the morning wasn't over yet. "The morning papers have arrived. Shall I bring them to you?"

Gaia nodded absently, not sparing more than a glance for the man. Boy, really. For as long as she could remember, her mother had hired assistants like him. Boys who wouldn't meet her eyes and jumped to do her mother's bidding, because if they didn't, they'd be out on their ear and Mother would have a new boy in his place. Maybe Gaia would replace the endless parade of boys with a woman next time. At least she wouldn't be embarrassed when the woman picked up her dry cleaning. Harrison, though…the few times he'd looked at her, when her mother was still alive, there'd been something in his eye that made her wonder if he was thinking…inappropriate thoughts. Or was that Bradley, the previous one? She couldn't keep track of them all. They all looked so alike. And it's not like she'd ever be interested in a man of their type, anyway.

Flicking open the newspaper, Gaia grinned as she

beheld the headline photo. Now there was a man who was definitely any woman's type. Why had rock star Jay Felix made the news this time? Hadn't his band broken up? Not that she cared about the rest of his band. Just the ripple of muscles on his shirtless torso, that tempting V between his hips that vanished into the waistband of his pants…

Gaia shook herself. It had been too long since her last holiday. She needed to relieve a little tension, if a blurry newspaper photo of a man could get her hot under the collar. A holiday somewhere private, where she could have a little liaison with no strings attached, and no rumours to follow her home. Not this week, though.

Her eyes returned to the headline article that accompanied the picture, announcing that Jay Felix would be sponsoring some major travel convention in the city next month, and he was offering a stay at his favourite private resort as a door prize. A private resort? That might suit her, Gaia mused, scanning the article for details of the resort's location.

The prize included flights to Broome and transfers to Romance Island Resort in the Buccaneer Archipelago. No, that couldn't be right…could it? Lorikeet Island was in the Buccaneer Archipelago. It was too big a coincidence. It couldn't be the same island group.

She searched for the resort on her computer, only to discover that Romance Island was only a few kilometres from Lorikeet Island. A short boat trip, or helicopter flight. Perhaps it might be possible to combine business with pleasure. If only the rock star would be in residence when she arrived…

Gaia picked up her phone and dialled Harrison's

extension.

"Yes, ma'm?" he answered.

Ma'am. Now she felt old. She wasn't even thirty yet.

"Arrange travel for me to Romance Island Resort next week. I want a whole week there, with a helicopter at my disposal. Their best accommodation. With privacy. No, make it two weeks."

"Yes, ma'am," he repeated.

Gaia gritted her teeth. "And you will call me Miss Vasse. Not ma'am."

"Yes, ma – uh, Miss Vasse."

She hung up without another word. It was definitely time to negotiate a merger between business and pleasure.

FOUR

Stewart's drawl made Gaia drowsy: "And once we have those in place, we can commence the shutdown. Decommissioning of the mine is estimated to take – "

"Who said anything about shutting down or decommissioning Lorikeet Island mine? We've barely scratched the surface of the ore deposit there!" Gaia glared.

"Your late mother understood that it was only a matter of time before the safety risks inherent in that seawall would require a shutdown. The environmental approvals alone would make building a new one impossible, or so expensive that it may as well be impossible. Particularly with the falling price of iron ore and the current state of the Chinese market," Stewart continued smoothly. His smile seemed particularly slimy as he added, "Your mother was fully prepared to cut her losses and close Lorikeet Island."

Not before hell froze over. Lorikeet Island was the basis

for her family's luck. No one would shut it down until every speck of useful ore was gone.

"What losses?" Gaia demanded.

Stewart paled. Oh, it was only slight, but Gaia knew him well enough to recognise when she had the man discomfited. Good.

"The infrastructure losses, of course, and the high cost of replacing them. Your mother – "

Gaia had heard enough. "My mother would never shut down a profitable mine. Especially not that one. And I'm her daughter, so neither will I. What about insurance? We pay enough for it. That should cover the costs of replacing the damaged buildings, as well as the mine itself. Our usual clients will need to know about the delays, and when they can expect normal production to resume. When do you estimate we can send out the next shipment of Lorikeet ore?"

Stewart stared. "Miss Vasse, I don't think you understand. The mine is under water. There's nowhere for the staff to stay. There will never be another shipment of ore from Lorikeet Island."

She stiffened. "I don't think you understand, Stewart. Vasse Prospecting and every mine it owns belongs to me. That means every important decision also comes down to me. Maybe you used to bully my mother into bad decisions, but that won't work with me. I am not my mother, and I'm not my grandfather, either. What was impossible for them is a morning's work for me. If I say the mine stays open, then it stays open."

"Good luck with that," he sneered. "Without accommodation, you won't have any staff. Lorikeet Island is one of the most remote mines in the world. Have you ever been there? Fourteen metre tides, cyclones that flatten everything in their path, and the only way in or out of there is by plane, and the storm damaged the air strip. You can't fly people in from town every day. The only reason Lorikeet Island stayed open as long as it has is because of the old resort accommodation your mother bought out back in the eighties. And what's left of that is under a couple metres of mud. So unless you have another hotel approved and ready to go on that island, it'll be a decade before you dig up anything else there. Just because you're a Vasse, doesn't mean you understand this business, little girl. Your mother was twice the businesswoman you'll ever be, and she couldn't hold a candle to her father. Why don't you go for another one of your little secret holidays that you think no one knows about? Drink cocktails and cavort with cabana boys like you usually do, while you leave running a billion-dollar business to those of us who know what we're doing."

Harrison. The spineless twerp was a spy for Stewart. His days were numbered.

"Maybe I will," Gaia spat, deciding not to tell Stewart about the real motives behind her planned trip north. "And when I get back, we'll discuss the future of Lorikeet Island. And your future with my company."

Stewart snorted, then left without another word.

Arrogant ass, she thought, fixing her gaze on the photograph of her and Mother. How did Mother put up with him so long? Mother had been one of the world's richest women, if not the richest, and all that now belonged to her. Mother hadn't made all that money by being an idiot. But if she'd been bullied by Stewart all this time…

Gaia shook her head. She wasn't her mother. No man would ever get the best of her.

She'd go to the Buccaneer Archipelago and see Lorikeet Island for herself, then regroup at the resort as she worked out how best to proceed with rebuilding her family's flagship mine. All she needed was somewhere for her staff to stay…

What had Stewart said about a resort? Another hotel approved and ready to go, as though he thought that was impossible. Perhaps it was, but what about one that was already built? Romance Island Resort, for instance.

Let Stewart think she was messing around with cabana boys. Instead, she'd stage the coup of the century and acquire the resort. Who would say no to the richest woman in the world?

No one, that's who.

FIVE

"What did you say your name was again?" a vague-sounding female voice asked.

"Gaia Vasse," she snapped, almost spitting the words into her telephone. What kind of idiot hadn't heard of her?

"Can you spell that, please?"

Gritting her teeth, Gaia did as requested, before the useless girl's reply was drowned out by another woman's shouting.

"You're not going because you announced on national television that we've opened the resort to terrorists. I've had ASIO sniffing around all week, wanting to see our guest lists, while our IT guys report almost daily hacker attacks. It's unheard of. What possessed you to say something so stupid?"

She sounded English, though her accent wasn't the refined sort Gaia preferred. No, this woman was as common as they came. One of the hotel staff, then. Definitely not a guest.

An Aussie male voice piped up, more annoyed than angry. "I said we welcomed guests of all nationalities and religions. Anyone who found it too cold in Russia or too hot in Syria would find Romance Island Resort a perfect sanctuary where their privacy is our priority. Tell me what about that makes it sound like I'm inviting terrorists to stay here!"

"That's exactly what I'm talking about. Every word makes it sound that way, and you don't get it! That's why I'll manage the media for the resort from now on. I don't have time to go to Perth, but now some ASIO Agent Dunn calls me every day until I fly down so he can interrogate me. No way are you going anywhere near that convention. You'll only make matters worse. Leave the business side of things for those of us who know what we're doing. Why don't you just go back to banging every fangirl you can find and let me do my job?"

"Flavia isn't a fangirl." The man's voice was reproachful.

"Fine, go back to banging whoever, then. Some of us have to work."

"Oh, Ms Lane?" the girl on the other end of the phone simpered.

"It's Vasse, not Lane," Gaia snapped.

The girl ignored her. "Ms Lane, I have Guy Vast on the phone for you."

"Who?" A sigh. "I'll take it in my office. Thanks, Philly."

The idiot receptionist was named for a horse? It figured. She wouldn't last more than five minutes in Vasse Prospecting. If the three people Gaia had just heard were an example of the incompetence of the staff at the resort, it would be hers within the week. Gaia smiled.

"Putting you through now," the girl announced, and her irritating voice was replaced with ringing.

"Hello, this is Xan Lane," the bored Englishwoman answered.

"I asked to be put through to the hotel manager," Gaia replied icily.

"That's me," the woman said easily. "I thought this was about a Mr Vast. Are you his assistant? Our receptionist should be able to handle all your booking requests."

"I'm no one's assistant," Gaia snapped. "My name is Gaia Vasse, and I'm interested in buying your hotel."

Silence, broken by a smooth, "What a lovely surprise, Miss Vasse. My condolences on the loss of your mother."

At least she recognised the name, and knew who she was. That was a start.

Xan continued, "But I'm afraid the resort is no longer for sale. The new owner took possession in January."

As if Gaia only bought properties listed on the open market. "Five months is hardly enough time to get attached to the place. Or for you to get accustomed to the change in management. I assure you, this is the best offer you'll ever get for the place. Especially with the proposed mine extension on your doorstep."

More silence. "You're planning on expanding the mine at Lorikeet Island? I'd understood from Mr Stewart last week that the shutdown team would be here as soon as the dry season starts. He made sure to assure me that the increased shipping traffic wouldn't impact on the resort or disturb our guests. This is a very exclusive resort, Miss

Vasse, as I'm sure you'd appreciate. The sort of place people like yourself choose for their holidays."

For all her common accent, the hotel manager wasn't too bad at talking business. Not in Gaia's league, though. "So I understand. Which is why I'll be flying up to inspect it for myself. We should meet in person to discuss the proposed sale of the resort."

Xan coughed. "You really should discuss this with the owner, not me, Miss Vasse. He has his own plans for the place. I just manage it, and I'll continue to do that, regardless of who owns the resort."

A possible future employee. One who knew what she was doing. Gaia restrained herself from rubbing her hands in glee. "Oh, I think we should keep it between us businesswomen. When we've worked out all the details, then you can bring my proposal to the owner as a done deal. No need to bother him just yet."

"If you say so, Miss Vasse. I'll get Philly to arrange the meeting. I look forward to it."

As she ended the call, satisfaction bloomed in Gaia's chest. She'd give the woman increased shipping traffic. A mine shutdown was nothing compared to an expansion. By the time she was done explaining the changes to the hotel manager, the woman would hand her the resort at a bargain price, because no guest would want to stay in a mining port. She could move her staff in next month.

SIX

On the screen, a bride glided down the church aisle on what Gaia presumed was her father's arm. All eyes, phones and flashing cameras turned toward the veiled image of virginity. A collective sigh sounded as the older man lifted the veil and kissed his daughter's cheek. Bridesmaids scuttled around her, settling her veil beneath her pinned curls. The groom's triumphant leer told the world that he didn't care for the veil or the dress, but the naked girl beneath them, who he intended to do all sorts of things to as soon as possible.

The girl ducked her head in response, as if to hide her blush. She turned slightly to scan the congregation, a lost look on her face as if she'd suddenly realised she might not like losing her virginity.

The priest clicked on his microphone and cleared his throat.

The bride stiffened, as if she'd suddenly grown a spine, and she snatched the microphone out of the man's hands. "I don't want to do this," she said in a breathy voice.

Laughter erupted from the congregation.

"But thanks to this arsehole, I have to," she continued.

All laughter died.

"He wanted us to save ourselves for marriage. He swore if I would, he'd do the same. Did you, James?" She turned to the groom.

"Of course, Vee," he drawled.

"Lying through your teeth in a church, you lying sack of shit. Just like you said you'd call off the wedding when I told you I knew you'd slept with a prostitute a few weeks ago. You can stick this wedding up your arse, James, just like you did to her." The bride drew her bouquet over her shoulder, then let it fly. The ball of roses hit the ceiling in an explosion of white petals, before landing among the congregation. A scuffle broke out, but the noise was muffled by the bride with the microphone as she added, "Fire it up, Vi. Show them what he did."

A projector screen behind the altar burst into a blur of colour, which resolved into a sordid scene between a couple who looked like they were having sex on a table.

"But I did it for you, Vee. She was showing me how to give you a good time!" the groom wailed.

"You aren't worth my time." The bride kneed him in the groin, then stormed out of the church.

Harrison laughed so hard he had to wipe his eyes. That's when he noticed Gaia standing behind him. "Have you seen this?" he asked her. "It's the funniest thing I've ever seen. The video of him having sex went viral a few weeks ago, and it's like the next chapter. It's been up for a couple of days and already it's had over two million views."

Gaia didn't crack a smile. "I can see why. You've already watched it four times. On company time."

Harrison's face fell. "Nah, I'm on my lunch break."

"It doesn't matter. Company policy on using office computers for pornographic material says it's instant dismissal," Gaia said steadily. "Goodbye, Harrison."

Harrison waved at the screen. "But…that's not pornography! It's a wedding! Everyone was still dressed!"

"The sex tape on the screen looked pretty pornographic to me. We can take it up with HR, if you like, and leave the definition up to them, or you can just resign." She kept her eyes on him. She wouldn't blink first.

Harrison hung his head. "I guess I could find another job in the next two weeks while I finish up here."

"I said instant dismissal. Pack your things and get out."

"But – " Harrison reconsidered and closed his mouth. He tucked his wallet and phone into his pockets, grabbed his coffee mug and slouched out.

Good riddance, Gaia thought. She hadn't expected getting rid of Harrison to be as easy as…the bride breaking up with the groom. If it had been her, she'd have set the guy up with the prostitute, to test his loyalty. After all, the cameraman with the viral videos had been so conveniently in the right place at the right time. That was no accident.

"You're nothing like your mother," Harrison spat, appearing in the doorway. He must have found his balls outside, or some sort of courage. "She never would have thrown out family."

"Are we related?" Distantly, through marriage, perhaps,

Gaia thought, but she didn't remember him from anywhere aside from the desk he'd just vacated.

"My father worked himself into an early death in your family's asbestos mines. I'm all Mum's got left, and the government won't pay for the medicine she needs to stay alive. She'll die if you fire me." He jutted a defiant chin for what Gaia suspected was the first time in his life.

She shrugged. "You should have thought of your mother when you chose to watch pornography in the office. At least you have the luxury of a mother who's still alive. I'm not wallowing because my mother is gone, or wasting my time watching other people having sex." She didn't mention that she had just done so – four times, in fact, as a familiar heat grew between her thighs. She wondered what it would be like to be taken over a table like that. It wasn't something any of her male partners had dared to do to her. Ugh. Was she seriously considering sex in such an uncomfortable position, without being in control? She needed to scratch that itch and soon.

"Bitch," Harrison snarled, then stomped out.

Gaia didn't deign to reply. He was beneath her, after all. Would she ever meet anyone who wasn't?

SEVEN

"More champagne, ma'am?" the air hostess asked. She didn't seem to care that the clashing combination of pink and orange on her uniform was hideous. Or perhaps she didn't know.

Gaia shook her head and the woman in the garish dress left her alone with her *Financial Review*. A glance out the window told her that they weren't in Broome yet, for the monotonous landscape of red rocks stretched from one horizon to the other. Not for the first time, it reminded her of the surface of Mars. Was that particular planet as rich in mineral resources as her own? If it was, the mining company who claimed it would be rich beyond its wildest dreams. There'd be no pesky environmental regulations, for there'd be no environment to ruin and rehabilitate afterwards. There'd be no such thing as minimum wages, either – she could bring in staff from whatever country she pleased, and pay them accordingly. No unions, no safety standards…Mars would make gold mines look insignificant in comparison.

The stewardess' voice startled her out of her Martian dreams: "Could you please stow your table, ma'am? We're about to commence our descent into Broome."

Broome. Mars could wait. First, she had this world to conquer. Then she could start on the next.

EIGHT

A man wearing shorts and knee socks carried her bags to the waiting helicopter. Gaia hadn't seen a grown man wear anything like it since she was a kid, and even then it was rare. He looked like an overgrown schoolboy. She hid her laughter behind her usual public mask, though, and followed him to her ride.

He started asking questions the moment they left the ground, but she refused to respond. Instead, she stared out the window, as red rock gave way to a riot of green that ended in white beach and aquamarine seas. The colours out here were enough to make her eyes water. Gaia donned her sunglasses to block out the unfamiliar glare. Perhaps she shouldn't have had that second glass of champagne on the flight up. Thank goodness she'd refused a third.

Aquamarine deepened to turquoise, dotted with rust-coloured islands frosted in green. None of them looked like paradise. In fact, many of them resembled the photos of Lorikeet Island, though without the buildings. Maybe that meant the vegetation hid rich ore bodies like the Lorikeet one. She wondered who owned the mining lease for them all. With luck, it was Vasse Prospecting. She needed to send a geology team out here to investigate, if no one had already.

"Approaching Romance Island now," the pilot said.

Gaia tapped him on the shoulder. "I want to fly over Lorikeet Island on the way."

He shot her a puzzled glance. "Lorikeet isn't on the way."

"It is on mine. I'm not landing at the resort until I've seen the damage at Lorikeet Island for myself." Gaia drew herself up. "I understood that my assistant booked your services for the length of my stay here. You're at my disposal. And I say we fly to Lorikeet Island."

"Yes, ma'am," he drawled, sketching a sloppy salute. "I can do a flyover for you, but there's nowhere safe to land at the moment. The helipad's underwater right now."

"Fine," she snapped. Was it just her imagination, or was his show of respect more a mockery than the real thing? Perhaps he didn't know who she was. She'd enlighten him later, when she had a better view of his face, so she could enjoy his horrified expression.

After some time with only the sound of the helicopter blades, the pilot broke the silence. "There's your island up ahead, Ms Vasse. Where your mine used to be."

Gaia stared in stunned disbelief. Sandwiched between steel-grey seas and scudding clouds, the island looked as uninhabited as all the others they'd passed on the way here.

But how could that be? She'd seen pictures of houses over half the island…an air strip…a swimming pool…not to mention the sea wall. Now, there was nothing to show for nearly seventy years' work. How could one storm obliterate her family's whole history?

"Fly lower," she instructed.

Without warning, the pilot banked and the island loomed closer to the side window before he straightened out to hover over a red slope that looked like it had just been cleared of vegetation. "This is what's left of the camp, after your airstrip turned mudslide and engulfed it," he said, then pointed out the window. "At low tide, you can still see what remains of the sea wall, but now even that's under water. It was a disaster waiting to happen and the guys who worked here were glad to be evacuated before it did. They flew out yesterday, or the pubs in town would still be full." He stared at the island. "End of an era, they said. The end of Lorikeet Island mine."

"It's not the end. I will never shut down Lorikeet Island. Not as long as I live and breathe," Gaia insisted.

The pilot snorted. "Looks pretty well shut down to me, and your mining crew think the same. You might want to let them know not to start looking for new jobs yet, or start retraining them as divers. There are a few good dive schools in town I can recommend."

It wasn't until she caught his grin that she realised he was joking.

"It's no laughing matter. The mine will reopen. Just watch me."

"Good luck, Ms Vasse. You're going to need it. Have you seen enough, or do you want to hang around here for a bit, planning bigger and better for the future? I don't know about you, but the resort's pub is a whole lot more hospitable for that sort of thing. It even has beer."

Gaia frowned in distaste. Beer was for common men, not her. She preferred a fine white wine, or a bottle of champagne. The resort had better serve more than just beer if they intended to keep her among their clientele.

NINE

The pilot lifted down her bag and set it on the paving beside the helipad. "If you need me, get Reception to give me a call. They know how to reach me."

Gaia stared at him. "You mean you're not staying here? What happened to being at my disposal? I expressly asked –
"

"My baby and I are at your service during your stay here, but I live on the mainland. At the pearl farm. You need us, just call, and I'll be here within a half-hour. You're on Broome time now, Ms Vasse. Welcome to the Kimberleys." With a jaunty wave, he jumped back into his helicopter and slammed the door.

Gaia backed away from the spinning blades, looking from her bags to the helicopter and back again. "What about my things? Aren't you going to carry them inside for me?"

He evidently hadn't heard her over the engine, as he continued grinning as he lifted off the ground, taking his aircraft out of sight over the palm trees. The man had no respect whatsoever. She wished she'd gotten his name so she could report him to his superiors.

A blonde girl came flying around the corner, breathless with excitement. Or from running, Gaia decided, though there was definite excitement. "Oh, Miss Vasse, welcome to Romance Island Resort! It's such an honour to have you here." When Gaia didn't respond, the girl continued, "I'm Philomena, but you can call my Philly. I can't believe it. I've barely been here a week and I get to meet you. Let me take your bags." She struggled with them, but still managed to lift them off the ground before staggering off the way she'd come.

After a moment's hesitation, Gaia decided to follow her. A large building became visible through the palm trees – all two storeys of it. Presumably, this was the hotel proper, where she planned on putting her staff. It probably wasn't as compact as the standard camp accommodation they were used to, but if the luxury fittings were part of the price she paid for the resort, at least it would save her the cost of a renovation for a few years until the miners wore everything out. Then she could replace everything with more utilitarian facilities, and use the resort as the labour camp for all the nearby islands.

"How many rooms does the hotel have?" Gaia demanded.

"Um…around fifty, I think," Philomena said. "Plus the villas, of course."

Fifty wasn't enough for the number of staff she needed

to house. With such luxury accommodation, they could share, she decided. A place like this would have king sized beds, which were easy to separate into two singles. Once those reached the end of their useful life, she'd replace them with bunk beds. A temporary measure, the staff would be told, until they no longer asked about it and accepted their working conditions. After all, most other mines were laying off staff. They'd consider themselves lucky to have a job here.

"Of course, you're in the jewel of the Pearls, as you'd expect. Villa Maxima." The girl beamed as if the names should mean something to Gaia.

"When is my meeting with the manager?" Gaia asked, bringing the conversation back to business. At least, business she understood. Pearls were a business for some people, after all.

"Which manager?"

"The manager of the hotel!" Gaia snapped.

"Oh. I'll have to check." Philomena propped open a door with one of Gaia's bags, then followed her into the hotel foyer. "Let me get you checked in, with your ID and everything, and then I'll page the manager."

Ten minutes later, with an uncomfortable band clipped to her wrist that Philomena assured her she had to wear as her access pass to the resort facilities, as well as its being the key to her room, Gaia settled in one of the foyer couches, refusing to leave until the manager came to greet her.

TEN

After five minutes of waiting, Gaia was furious. After fifteen, she was livid. By thirty-seven, she wasn't entirely sure what she was any more, but a strange slapping sound distracted her.

A bloke wearing nothing but soaking wet board shorts, water cascading down his ripped body like he'd just stepped from the ocean, ambled up to the reception desk. His wet feet slapped on the tiles with every step. He pointed at his wristband, which looked just like the one Gaia now wore. "What's the emergency?" he asked Philomena. "I don't see the building on fire. The cyclone season is almost over, and Shou can't have crashed his helicopter again because I saw it take off while I was having my afternoon swim."

"No, it's…um…" Philomena began in a carrying whisper, before pointing at Gaia. "She asked to see the manager."

The man shrugged, sending a fresh trickle down his back muscles. "So get Xan."

"Ms Lane left for Perth this morning. She won't be back for a week and she said if anyone wanted to see the manager, to get you. So, I got you."

"You summoned me from my swim for her, because she's an emergency?" He turned to stare at Gaia, as if he didn't care how rude he looked. "Not my kind of emergency. She's a four, maybe a five, tops. Give her the number of the escort service in town. It's the wet season. I'm sure they have a gigolo free for her."

A four? Maybe a five? Gaia had never been so insulted in her life. She jumped to her feet. "I asked to see the manager because I made an appointment."

He strode over so he stood a metre from her. "Not with me, lady. You're not my type."

"Are you gay, Mr Felix?" she asked coldly.

He didn't seem the slightest bit offended. "I haven't met a man yet who made me think so. But women...I love women. Like I said, though, you're not my type. I like my girls young and pretty."

"I'm only two years older than you!" she blurted out.

Jay laughed. "Still doesn't make you pretty." He strode out the door, whistling.

Gaia wasn't sure whether she wanted to run after him and tackle him to the ground or beat him over the head. She couldn't get the image of water trickling down his chest and abs, following that tempting V down into his pants, clinging to what she could see was a sizeable...

Dick. He was a complete dick. Making her wait, then insulting her. Jay Felix wasn't worth her time, no matter how perfect the man's body was.

Gaia marched up to the reception desk. "Get me the hotel manager on the phone. The real hotel manager, not that man. Now."

Philomena nodded and dialled.

ELEVEN

Gaia smiled as she sipped from her glass of well-chilled champagne, settling deeper into the couch of her villa as her gaze settled on the eastern horizon, where Lorikeet Island lay. The sunset set the cliffs aglow, making the horizon look like a wall of fire over the water. Her island and her mine – those very cliffs were the ones her grandfather had mined back in the fifties.

The hotel manager had been properly apologetic, promising to arrange a dinner meeting for her with the owner, after she'd spoken to him to make sure he understood not only who she was, but how important her offer was.

He. Typical. There were too many businessmen in the world, and not enough businesswomen. Of course, that did make her job easier sometimes. Men frequently underestimated her. Once they'd realised she wasn't an easy conquest, they became so lost that negotiations inevitably went her way. The world was her oyster – one that always gave her pearls. Not that she was particularly fond of an old lady's jewel – she preferred gold, unsullied by any sparkly, attention-seeking stone that drew the eye away from the valuable metal. Pearls weren't even truly stones.

She drained her glass, then poured another. She'd need a little extra alcohol to help her relax after this afternoon's irritation. Not to mention the disappointment that was Jay Felix. He mustn't have known who she was, Gaia consoled herself. When she saw him again, she'd be certain to tell him, so he knew who he'd insulted, and he could fully appreciate the opportunity he'd lost.

She checked her watch. Still a couple of hours to go. She might take a relaxing swim from her private beach before returning to dress for dinner. She certainly intended to make an impression on the owner. One he wouldn't soon forget.

TWELVE

Xan scowled at her phone. The chairman of Vasse Prospecting – in fact, the whole Vasse family – were an unpleasant lot. Snobbish and uppity at best; downright litigious at worst. She'd preferred to deal with James Stewart on anything to do with Lorikeet Island. He wasn't any less mercenary – he wanted the mine to make money as much as the Vasse girl and her late mother – but he was a damn sight more pleasant and down-to-earth. The few minutes she'd spent on the phone to Gaia Vasse made her suspect the girl thought anyone less wealthy than the Queen would be beneath her notice.

That's why she'd left the girl to Jay. Jay irritated everybody and, sure enough, he'd offended her the moment he met her. He'd done such a good job that the girl had been livid, as opposed to just being annoyed enough to leave the island alone. She'd screeched about lawyers and finished up with a blistering lecture on professionalism, most of which seemed to be about kissing her well-polished arse.

Still, the girl did have one ace up her sleeve – the massive media pull that came from owning shares in a lot of the news companies. A few words in the right ears and Little Miss Vasse could make the media tide turn against the resort. Xan's whole advertising campaign would fall flat, drowned out by whatever dirt Vasse's paid reporters could dig up. All she'd have to say was that her mine was expanding and the resort would be in the middle of a major shipping channel. Lies, of course, but by the time anyone printed anything else, the damage would be done.

So, against her better judgement, Xan did what she'd promised Gaia: she rang Jay to set up a dinner meeting so the two could discuss Gaia's plans.

Jay didn't answer his phone, so she asked Philly to page him. Less than five minutes later, Xan's phone rang.

"Hel – "

Jay cut her off. "This better not be about that rich bitch in the foyer."

Xan tried not to laugh. For once, she agreed with him. "I'm calling about Gaia Vasse. She's the chairman of Vasse Prospecting, the owner of Lorikeet Island Mine next door to the resort, and she has a business proposition for you."

"Bullshit. She wants me in her bed. She looked me up and down like a piece of meat."

This time, she couldn't stifle her laughter. "Were you wearing anything at the time?"

"My board shorts. They covered all the essentials. I was swimming when Reception paged me. They said it was urgent, so I didn't stop to put on a bloody suit." Jay laughed. "Oh, it was urgent all right. She was panting like a bitch in heat. I told her to get a gigolo in town, because she was too old and ugly for me."

No wonder the girl had been angry. Xan probably would have felt insulted, too, if she hadn't known that his type seemed to mostly include girls who fell at his feet for the opportunity for a night with him. Flavia and Phuong had been exceptions to that, of course, but Gaia definitely wasn't his type.

"I promised her she'd get to meet with the owner and discuss her business proposal at seven this evening. Over dinner. I've already booked a private dining room, so it'll just be the two of you." It already sounded more like a date than a business meeting. "All I ask is that you hear her out, possibly get a copy of what she's proposing, and don't agree to anything. Not verbally, and definitely not in writing. Even if nothing's binding without Jo or my signature, she'll still try to hold you to whatever it is. She's got more lawyers than you do."

"And if she tries to rip my clothes off?" Jay grumbled.

Xan grinned. "I imagine you're used to that, rock star. Do whatever you usually do. But if you end up doing her on the dining table, I don't want to hear about it."

"I can name fifty women I'd rather do on the dining table instead of her."

Xan sighed. She didn't want to know that, either. "Just remember that she has a lot of clout with the media. If you annoy her enough, she might make trouble with the press."

Jay laughed. "That's the last thing I'd worry about. I have no secrets from the media — they have everything from naked photos from when I was arrested for lewd conduct in Sydney through to…fuck, I dunno. What's another picture of my bare arse in the entertainment news? Old news."

Before Xan could give him any more advice, Jay ended the call.

She sighed. It was his resort, after all. She just managed the place. Somehow, she wasn't sure he had the full measure of Gaia Vasse just yet. She prayed that he did before anything bad happened.

THIRTEEN

Dinner was scheduled for seven, so at precisely eleven minutes past, Gaia swept into the private dining room wearing a dress from the resort collection some Australian designer had begged to give her. She hadn't found an occasion to wear it to yet, as the white linen and lace seemed too casual for a formal occasion, yet too pretty for work. Tonight, it was perfect.

She produced a gracious smile for her host, only to discover that she was alone. So much for being fashionably late in order to make an entrance. The rude owner wasn't anywhere to be seen.

Mentally, she dropped the price she was willing to pay for his resort. How dare he keep her waiting. He was worse than that rude rock star, whose rippled muscles could rot off before she'd ever think of…

"You again." Jay strolled in, grabbed the bottle of

champagne from the ice bucket and sloshed some into a glass before offering her the bottle. "Drink?"

Gaia shook her head irritably. "Get out. This is a private meeting and you're not invited."

Jay yanked out the owner's chair and slouched on it. He gulped from his glass, then grinned. "You mean there really are gigolos in town, and you booked one this fast? You must be really gagging for it. No wonder you couldn't take your eyes off me in Reception this afternoon. I know I'm hot, but you looked like you wanted to eat me alive. Not my kind of kink, if you know what I mean." He winked and drank some more.

Gaia felt furious heat rising in her body. Of course it was anger. Not attraction to this awful man. "I said get out. I'm here to meet with the owner of this resort, not some – "

"Rich rock star who just bought the place?" he supplied. She wanted to wipe the lazy grin off his face. "Who do you think owns the fucking resort? This is my piece of paradise, Gaia. Even a rock star needs a retreat, in between touring and recording and shit."

She fought to hide her shock. "There's no need to swear," she managed to say.

He set his glass down and leaned across the table. "Yeah, there fucking is. This is my island. My home. And I don't take kindly to some nosy neighbour coming to my place and ordering me around. Summoning me from my swim. Telling me to get out of my own dining room. Or telling me I can't say whatever I fucking want in my own fucking home. So what if you own the island next door? I've seen what you've done with the place, and it looks fucked up. We had to help the miners get off the island, so they came here by jet boat because by the time the evacuation order came, the wind was too strong for anything to fly. Fifty blokes in my pub who had a lot to say about you and yours, none of it good. Most dangerous mine in Australia, they said, placing bets on whether the sea wall would come down in this storm or the next. They were glad to be gone because they considered themselves lucky to be alive. So how about you tell me how a hard-hearted bitch like you gets to play with men's lives just to make more money, while the rest of us have to obey the safety laws?"

Gaia stared. "I didn't know," she whispered.

Jay cupped his hand around his ear. "I didn't hear that. And from what I do hear, it's no fucking excuse. It's called negligence."

"I didn't know," she repeated, moistening her dry mouth. Now she wanted that drink. "I only inherited the mine from my mother last week. I wasn't managing it before then. She…she killed people?"

Jay snorted. "Nah, she didn't kill anyone, but not for lack of trying. The safety standards over there were shit. I'm surprised the sea wall held that long. I watched it crumble from here. The sea reclaimed her own."

Gaia didn't know what to say.

Jay didn't seem to mind. "And now you're here, trying to order me around like you own the place. My hotel manager tells me you have a business proposition for me. One I should hear. Now, I take her advice because that's what I pay her for, but even she's not stupid enough to order me around. You haven't said anything that interests me yet. So, what's this proposition that's so important?"

A waiter brought in their entrées, giving Gaia a chance

to collect her thoughts. She glanced at her plate. Artistic swirls of something with a small, caviar-topped mound in the middle. Properly presented food, whatever it was, so she dipped her fork and sampled it. Deeming the food acceptable, she shrugged her shoulders and took a little more.

Jay hadn't touched his. He sat there expectantly, his eyes not leaving her. "Why are you here?"

Because she'd seen a panty-melting picture of him in the paper. Gaia tried to swallow but choked instead. She grabbed her glass of wine and used it to calm her coughing.

"I want your island," she said hoarsely.

Jay burst out laughing, slapping his hand so hard against the table that the glasses shook. "You're joking, right?"

She shook her head.

"You're not mining my island, turning it into a sandpit beside a toxic waste dump while you work men to death here. No fucking way."

Gaia wanted to shrink away from his anger, but she couldn't. Her fortune depended on her courage. She summoned a sneer. "Of course not. There's nothing on this sand cay worth mining. It's the buildings I want. I need somewhere for my staff to stay while they rebuild Lorikeet Island." She avoided his eyes and turned her attention to finishing her food.

"Then you can book them in like any other guests. You don't need to meet with me for that. My hotel manager can discuss rates with you. Maybe even give you a bulk discount." He threw his fork down with a clatter on his empty plate.

The sound summoned a waiter, who cleared away the

dishes while Gaia waited. Finally, they were alone again.

"That's not acceptable. I'm not paying for common miners to stay in luxury accommodation. We'll convert the rooms to camp style rooms and bring in our own cooks..."

"Like fuck you will!" Jay glared. "This is a luxury resort and it'll fucking stay that way while I own it. We have chefs, not cafeteria cooks." He waved at the main course now sitting before him.

Gaia fought to keep her patience. "That's why I propose purchasing the resort. The changes will occur after the property has changed hands."

Jay swallowed a large mouthful of food. "No changes and no changing hands. I'm not selling."

"Mr Felix, when the mine reopens, and it will, we'll be increasing production as we plan to mine several of the other nearby islands. One ship a week will become one a day. Dredgers will circle your island, making your pristine wilderness into a tiny oasis in the middle of a busy mining port. All the traffic will scare away the fish, the birds and any other wildlife that makes this reserve so unique, until there's nothing left. No one will want to stay here. Your resort will go bankrupt and then I'll move in and buy it from the receivers at a bargain price." She flashed a smug smile. "Be reasonable. Mine is the best offer you'll ever get for this place."

What unsettled her most was Jay's answering smile. "You do that, and I'll close down the resort. No staff, no guests, just me and maybe some temporary staff when I'm here. And an environmental monitoring crew, to record the damage until I take you to court."

"My lawyers are the best," Gaia insisted. "You can't

possibly win."

"I don't have to," Jay replied. "All I have to do is get enough media attention for the court case to reach the ears of the environmental regulators in Perth. Maybe Canberra, too. And the protestors. Do you even know how many endangered species we have up here? Dolphins. Whales. Birds. Some kind of lizard. And if you screw with the ocean, you'll have the fishing lobby up in arms as well. Don't underestimate the power of fishermen in Western Australia. There's the commercial ones who are rich enough to challenge you on their own, but everyone who takes a rod or a tinny out on the weekend has a vote. Everyone fishes in WA. And politicians know that." His eyes darkened. "You forgot about the local Aboriginal communities, too. They might not have had much power when Lorikeet Island mine opened, but now they own every damn island in the whole Buccaneer Archipelago. Nothing happens on these islands without their say-so. Me and the guys at the pearl farm, we have an agreement. A lease with them, with conditions, but they're still pissed off about losing Lorikeet Island. They won't let you have any of the others."

"But…that's bad business. Closing your business indefinitely on the chance of getting public support to stop me? It could take years. Think of all the money you'll lose!"

"I'm a rock star, not a hotel tycoon. My business is making music. If I run out of cash, I'll just record another album, or go on tour again. My fans fucking love me. When you and your mine are gone, my island will still be waiting for me. Even if I have to wait until I retire. You're the one whose business will be in trouble when half the state decides they hate you and what you're doing up here. And I'll make sure they know what's going on."

She shrugged. "We'll see. Money can make any problem go away."

It was Jay's turn to choke. With laughter. "What fucking tower have you been living in where they let you believe THAT?" He wiped his mouth with the back of his hand. So crude. "You can buy things. Not people. Not opinions. And not my fucking island."

Gaia forced herself to smile, even as her heart sank. "We'll see, Mr Felix."

Another snort. "No, you'll see, baby. My answer's no and no amount of begging will change my mind."

"I've never begged in my life!"

Jay winked. "Maybe that's where you're going wrong. You should try getting down on your knees some time. A bloke can be a bit more friendly when you do that, instead of ordering him around."

Gaia frowned to hide the tumult inside. She should be angry. She should be furious at this man for refusing her and even suggesting she do anything for him on her knees. But a thrill twisted in her belly, making her wonder what it might be like to get friendly with this man. He was a bastard, but his body combined with that voice...

For the first time in her life, she lowered her eyes and forced herself to eat the rest of her meal in silence. She wouldn't give him the satisfaction of a reply. At least, not until he offered her some sort of satisfaction first.

FOURTEEN

When the next day dawned, Gaia wished the sun would go back to sleep so she could, too. Her night had been filled with dreams of Jay Felix and the things she wanted him to do to her. At this rate, she'd have to buy herself a marital aid…a…vibrator, like some lonely spinster who couldn't find a partner to share her bed for a night.

Gaia shook herself. No. Absolutely not. A billionaire didn't need a battery-operated substitute for a man. She merely snapped her fingers and men came running. She'd find a member of the hotel staff willing to fulfil her wishes and Jay wouldn't be a temptation for her any more. Admittedly, it didn't look like this place had a pool, but surely there were some attractive young men working here. The resort uniform of shorts and short-sleeved shirts certainly gave a girl the opportunity to get a good look at the available talent.

The doorbell chimed, alerting her that her breakfast had arrived. Gaia slipped into a robe – hers, not the hotel's – and made her way to the door to allow the room service attendant to make his delivery.

He had nicely toned calves beneath his shorts, she noted, deciding that the rest of him looked suitably fit for her tastes. He certainly wasn't as skinny as Harrison, that was for sure.

"Will there be anything else, ma'am?" he asked.

Gaia favoured him with a seductive smile. "How might a single girl go about acquiring some male company for an evening here at the resort?"

To her horror, the young man laughed, then tried to hide it with a cough. When he'd managed to compose himself, he said, "You might want to try the hotel bar, the Jungle. It won't be open until the afternoon, but most resort guests like to watch the sunset from there as they grab a few drinks."

She hadn't expected him to be too bright, but most male staff at the other resorts she'd visited recognised a hint when they heard one. Evidently Australian resorts were different. Fine. She'd lay it on thick until he did understand. "And what if I'm not interested in the resort guests so much as the resort staff?"

His eyes turned cold. "Then you're out of luck, ma'am. The resort has strict rules about staff who fraternise with guests. It's grounds for instant dismissal."

Gaia waved away his worries. "How would they even know what happens in the privacy of a guest's villa?"

"Oh, they'd know, ma'am. The security here is the best, because that's what our guests expect. You enjoy your day."

Before she could say a single word in response, he hightailed out of the door.

Of all the impertinent…had a delivery boy actually refused to sleep with her? What was wrong with the people on this island? No respect whatsoever.

It must be the influence of the owner, Mr Rude Rock Star himself. Humph. Him and his talk of begging last night, after he'd refused to consider her offer for his island. She'd show him. Today, she'd confront him, turn on her most charming smile, and seduce him into her bed and out of his island.

Business was war, after all, and all was fair in love and war. That bastard was about to find out just what sort of ammunition she had in her arsenal…and he wouldn't be able to resist.

Because if he did…she'd become the first billionaire to buy a vibrator, and that definitely wasn't going to happen. Not to Gaia Vasse.

FIFTEEN

Gaia glanced in the mirror one last time. Did the wrap dress have to show quite that much cleavage? Perhaps she should wear it with one of her shell tops underneath, like she usually did. With so much of her breasts on display, she feared she looked like a common prostitute. Not that she'd ever seen a prostitute in the flesh, but she'd seen enough movies…

No. She'd seen the pictures of Jay with his many fans in the newspapers. After his concerts, he'd been photographed with girls showing far more flesh than the soft swell of her breasts on either side of this plunging v-neck. Most of them left very little to the imagination. If that was what Jay preferred, then perhaps she could flatter him just a little by giving him what he wanted. Then she'd be more likely to get everything she wanted…

Was his bottom as firm to the touch as it looked?

Gaia caught the blush blooming on her cheeks before she turned away from the mirror. It was now or never.

Doubting the directions the receptionist had given her, Gaia glanced at the names of the villas as she passed them. Hers was Maxima, beside Pinctada, then there was Albina, Margaritifera and Akoya, before the path led off into the jungle, without a sign to tell her whether it led to the owner's villa or not. She hesitated for a moment, before marching around the corner. A sign half-hidden behind a palm frond pointed the way to Villa Penguin. It looked official enough – but why on earth had the man called his house after a waddling bird, instead of a pearl, like all the others? Perhaps she'd ask him. Knowing Jay, he might not have had any reason at all for doing it. After all, if the man was crazy enough to close his business and wait until protestors had closed down her project...who knew what other insane ideas he had?

No. He couldn't be that crazy. His comments last night had been a bluff to get her to increase her price, she'd decided some time between one erotic dream and another.

There must be a point to the penguin, too. No one did silly things just for the hell of it.

Gaia marched up to his front door and rapped on the glass. She waited for a few seconds, hearing nothing from inside the villa, before knocking again. And again.

Still nothing.

She perched on one of the outdoor chairs on his veranda. Was he home and ignoring her, or was he somewhere else on the island? Perhaps she should try the windows. This villa looked like a smaller version of hers, which meant floor to ceiling windows with a view over the ocean or into the jungle. If she peeked through a few windows, she'd soon see if he was home or not. And if he was deliberately ignoring her…

Squeezing between the end of the veranda and a spiky shrub taller than she was, Gaia crept toward the first window. The blind was down, so she couldn't see a thing. She cursed under her breath and tiptoed further. The next window gave her a clear view of his empty kitchen. Was he still asleep at this hour of the morning? Surely he hadn't slept as badly as she had.

She bypassed the frosted glass door she guessed led to the bathroom, the same as the one in her villa. A path led from this door into the jungle – presumably, it ended at the beach like hers. The next window should be the master bedroom, if she'd guessed correctly. Gaia crossed the path, ducked behind a palm tree and peered through the window into a darkened room.

A firm hand grabbed her bottom. She jumped, but the grip tightened and didn't let go.

"Spying on resort guests is definitely against the rules," a male voice purred in her ear. "But if you tell me what you'd hoped to see, peering into my bedroom like that, maybe I'll see if I can give you a private show later that'll make all your dreams come true."

Her bottom grew uncomfortably hot under his hand. The heat spread rapidly to her core, reminding her of last night's lascivious dreams. "Unhand me," she demanded, but her voice was too breathless to sound properly imperious.

"Tell me why you're sneaking around my house, and I will."

Gaia twisted out of his grasp, so she could glare at him.

"I was looking for you." Too late, she remembered her intention of seducing him, but she forced herself to smile in the hope that it might help.

Jay spread his arms wide, once again showing off the fact that he wore nothing but a pair of wet board shorts. He must have come straight from a swim. "Here I am, baby. Have you thought about what I said last night and decided begging might be in your best interests? You wouldn't be the first."

No, she certainly wouldn't, Gaia thought, unable to take her eyes off his body. Why did she want this man so much? Damn it, she was here for his island, not him!

Fluttering her eyelashes and feeling ridiculous, she said, "I wanted to invite you to take a walk on my private beach with me."

Jay shrugged. "I can come for a walk, yeah." Not quite the enthusiasm she'd been hoping for, but at least he'd agreed.

Gaia led the way back to the main path, hearing the pad of Jay's bare feet following her. Then it faded.

She turned to find out why he'd stopped.

Jay stood on the path to Villa Akoya. "Where are you going? This is the shortest way to the beach. At least, it is as long as you're wearing those." He jerked his chin at her feet.

Gaia glanced at her heels. Did the man honestly expect her to go barefoot like him? While wearing this dress? Evidently, he knew nothing about fashion, but then, few men did, in her experience. She summoned a gracious smile. "Show me the way, then."

Her eyes zeroed in on his backside, outlined clearly by his wet, clinging board shorts. Actually, given their rosy colour and the shape of what was underneath, it made her think of the mango she'd eaten for breakfast that morning. Ripe, firm, but sweet enough to make her mouth water for more. Would he taste as sweet if she sank her teeth into him?

Gaia choked back a giggle at her own silliness. What kind of crazy woman bit into a man's bottom? Moreover, who thought he'd taste sweet? He'd taste salty, surely.

She looked up to meet Jay's quizzical gaze. "You right there?" he asked.

Gaia mumbled a non-committal reply, then swept past him before he spotted her rapidly heating cheeks.

She followed the sound of crashing waves to a narrow track leading off into the jungle. On her first step into the creamy sand, her shoe sank in to the sole, followed by the other one. She struggled out of the sand, only to sink again on every step. This track was torture. "I'd prefer to go back to my place and my private beach," she announced grandly.

Jay tramped past her, having no trouble with the sand beneath his bare feet. Big bare feet, too. "Why? All the private beaches are connected, with just a bit of jungle shielding each from the other. They're really just one long beach that ends at the top of the island. This is faster. Or it would be, if you'd take those stupid shoes off. You don't need shoes on this beach. The sand's like velvet, it's so fine. And still cool, seeing as the tide's only just heading out now."

Gaia's toes curled at the thought of taking her shoes off. She hadn't had a pedicure in weeks. There would be chips in her nail polish. No way was she revealing her imperfect toes to this man. It'd ruin everything she was trying to achieve. Not to mention, all the girls in the movies she'd skimmed over this morning kept their heels on. Seducing a man properly depended on wearing the right shoes.

Ignoring him, she slogged on.

"Have it your way, then." He overtook her almost effortlessly.

"Aren't you going to walk with me?" she demanded.

With an exaggerated sigh, he stopped. "That would be a lot easier if you weren't slower than most snails. Fine. I'll try to keep to your pace, but only if you tell me why you're insisting on going for a walk when you're evidently not enjoying it."

Gaia forced down her irritation as she attempted a coy smile. "After last night, I couldn't stop thinking about you. I wanted to spend more time with you. Alone." Eyelash batting. More eyelash batting. Couldn't forget the damned eyelash thing. And that pouty thing the girl did with her mouth…

Jay burst out laughing. "This seduction thing you've got going would be real cute, if it wasn't straight out of a bad porn film. You been watching the adult movie channel all night, drinking champagne and fantasising that Mr Moustachioed pool man was me?"

Gaia's mouth dropped open and she couldn't seem to close it. How had he known?

"You're not the first, baby, and you won't be the last, I'm sure. Can't say the same, though. I get so much of the real thing, I don't have time for fantasies." His grin left her in no doubt that he was telling the truth. His gaze slid from her face to the horizon. "Fact is, I've had so much sex lately, I'm taking a bit of a breather. My girl's so hot for me

I need some rest, if you know what I mean, so I'm performing at my peak for her."

Jay Felix had a girlfriend hidden away in his house, while he was out here with her? That explained the room with the blind pulled down. So that's why he wasn't interested in her right now. He had some little playboy bunny waiting to fulfil his every desire.

But that bunny was nobody compared to her.

"So where is she, then? This perfect playmate of yours?" Gaia spread her arms wide. "I don't see her. Just you, me and this romantic beach, begging for a bit of…action. What do you say?" She winked.

Jay laughed so hard he choked. "Shit, you should really lay off the movies. You know porn's not real, right? She's not here. She had some business to deal with back home, and she got delayed. As soon as the media shit storm's died down around her, we'll be hot and heavy again like you wouldn't believe. It's hard to believe she was a virgin the first time I had her, but she was. So much for chastity, though…once she starts, Flavia never wants to stop. She's the first girl I ever had who could wear me out, and that's saying something." His eyes turned misty. "Takes her half the night to manage it, though."

Half the night? Hours. What Gaia would give for hours in bed with Jay Felix… Dreamily, she took another step and splashed into water, coming to an abrupt halt. "What on earth?" She tried to pull her shoe free, but it was stuck fast in a shell-lined hole. A wave broke over her foot, filling her shoes with seawater. They'd be ruined.

"Crab hole," Jay said.

Crabs? As in live ones with claws? They were fine once

dead, steamed and garnished on her plate but…still alive?

Gaia tugged frantically at her foot, but the shoe was stuck fast. As if this wasn't bad enough, the rainclouds overhead took that moment to dump their cargo in a shower of stinging drops. Stuck, nearly shoeless and fast becoming soaked, she turned to Jay and begged, "Help me!"

"You didn't say the magic word."

She stared at him. An insolent grin curled his lips as he stood there with his arms folded, just out of her reach. The rain didn't seem to faze him at all. Of course it didn't. He was wearing a pair of wet board shorts, not designer clothing that was rapidly becoming as ruined as her shoes. She swiped at her brimming eyes, hoping he couldn't tell the difference between tears and rain. Her hand came away smudged grey. Now her makeup was running, too. This was a disaster.

"Please," she forced out through gritted teeth. When he didn't move, she wailed, "Please help me."

Still he stood there. "You know, you could just take your shoes off. It's just a quick run up the beach to shelter."

And leave them behind? Never. "Please help me."

"Fine. But you owe me." He lowered his head and barrelled into her, like the madman was trying to tackle her. The next thing she knew, she was lifted into the air, thrown over his shoulder like a doll, her bare feet kicking air.

"Put me down!" she demanded, struggling.

"Do you want my help or do you want me to leave you here? Quit wiggling and I'll help you home. If you knee me one more time, I'll drop you on the sand and you can find your own fucking way home."

Gaia took a deep breath and stilled. Yes, he'd thrown

her over his shoulder, but her body was screaming for more. She wanted him to carry her home and help her out of her wet clothes and have his way with her, over and over and over again and…

Her toes touched paving as he set her on her feet again. Gaia surveyed her surroundings and was shocked to see she was on the steps to her villa – right outside the frosted glass bathroom door.

She could scarcely breathe. No man had ever done that to her before. She wanted him to do it again and so much more.

"You're welcome," Jay said, before striding off. The pouring rain soon hid him from sight.

SIXTEEN

Jay Felix had someone else. He'd rejected her for someone else.

As Gaia scrubbed herself in the shower, she couldn't think of anything else but the mysterious girl. Jay appeared in the media with dozens of girls, but never had he been linked with just one. Had she missed the media statement somehow, while she'd been too busy dealing with work?

Slipping into dry clothes, Gaia found the number of her media manager and placed a call. She didn't wait for the woman to finish her greeting before Gaia barked, "Stephanie? I need you to prepare a brief for me on someone. I need to know everything about this girl who's currently dating Jay Felix."

"Jay Felix? You mean rock star Jay Felix? He's not with anyone that I know of. That'd be big news in the media, for sure, if that tomcat ever settled down. He makes Mick

Jagger look chaste, and the guy's not even thirty yet."

Gaia didn't have the patience to deal with Stephanie's shortcomings. "He said she's been the focus of media attention at the moment, so you must have heard of her. Flavia or Chastity or something. He said something about how he was her first, so you'd be looking for someone who hasn't been romantically linked with anyone famous until him. Find her, Stephanie. I want to know everything about her." And once she did, she could show Jay why the girl wasn't worthy of his time, and he should pick her instead.

"Flavia? Chastity? Never heard of a girl called that. Oh, there was that virginity auction girl a few months ago…her name was Chastity. But that's all died down now. I've never heard of someone called Flavia…unless it's that girl in the viral video…you must have seen it. But that has nothing to do with the rock star. Just a cheating groom who – "

Was Harrison not the only staff member who'd been watching that wedding video at work? "I don't care what you do. Find her, and find out everything there is to know about her. Send your report to my email. By tomorrow." Gaia terminated the call without a farewell.

SEVENTEEN

Stephanie had outdone herself, Gaia decided, as the perused the report over breakfast. The media manager had unearthed a gold mine of dirt on the girl. Not only was she the bride in the video that had cost Harrison his job, but the girl herself was no better than a common whore who'd sold her body for cash. To a certain rock star, in fact. No wonder the man didn't want to sell the resort if he could afford to pay a million dollars for a prostitute.

Time to take a different tack.

As if on cue, her phone rang. Gaia lifted the receiver to her ear. "Yes?"

"Ms Vasse, I have Mr Felix on the line for you, as requested," the receptionist said. A few soft beeps sounded, followed by the sound of someone breathing into the receiver. Not the receptionist.

"Hello, Jay," Gaia purred. "I have a proposition for

you."

"Another one? No, you can't have my island. No, you can't have me, either. And no, I don't want to take you for another walk on the beach while you're wearing stupid shoes."

Gaia gritted her teeth. The tide had taken her shoes, she'd found, when she returned to retrieve them. Why hadn't he taken a moment to pick them up for her after helping her? But she didn't say it. "Have you ever been to Lorikeet Island?" she asked instead.

"No. It can't beat Romance Island. That's why we have a resort and your island's a mining pit. Or it was." There was no mistaking the taunt in his tone.

She forced herself to stay calm. "I've arranged for a helicopter to take me out there today to assess the damage. I'd like you to come with me."

"Why would I want to do that?" he drawled.

If he wanted to be difficult, fine. She'd learned business negotiation techniques before she'd learned to read. Now she had his attention, she needed to get him interested. "I'd like to show you what my company is trying to save. The mine is only a small part of the island, and only one island out of over a thousand in the Buccaneer Archipelago. As long as the mine remains open, Vasse Prospecting protects the whole island group and much of the surrounding ocean. It's part of our operating conditions."

"I'm listening."

Good. Now she needed to arouse his desire to help her. "We've been protecting the islands for more than sixty years, when we started rehabilitating Lorikeet Island from the damage it sustained during World War II. It would still be bare rock if it weren't for my grandfather's vision. He dreamed of one day retiring on the island, which is why he allowed a resort to be built there, but he died before he could create the paradise he'd planned. My mother incorporated the resort into the mining camp so she could keep them maintained, respecting her father's wishes for the island. She never really liked the island, but I've always loved my grandfather's dreams. Except...I thought keeping it for himself is too selfish, when paradise should be shared with the world. What you've seen of Lorikeet Island so far is my mother's lack of vision. Let me show you what I have in mind."

She could hear his breathing, so she knew he was still there. Trapped in her spell. Good. Now for the final touch to overcome his doubt.

"Mr Felix, spend the day with me at Lorikeet Island today, and I swear, if you don't want to do business with me and help me achieve the future these islands deserve, I'll leave you and your island alone." Having delivered her killing blow, Gaia held her breath.

"If I don't want to make a deal with you by the end of today, you'll stop pestering me? If I just spend one day with you?"

"Yes." She wished she could see his face. By the time most men started repeating her offer, she knew she'd closed the deal, but Jay was an unknown quantity.

He sucked in a breath. "All right, then. "

Yes! Gaia wanted to cheer so loudly it would be heard at Lorikeet Island, but she restrained herself. "Meet me in the hotel foyer at ten, then. And bring your boots."

EIGHTEEN

Gaia hated her steel-capped boots. From the weight to the clomping sound they made with every step to the sheer hideousness of wearing work boots, she wasn't sure what was worse. Safety standards being what they were, though, she was dressed like a common miner. Long sleeved shirt and long cotton pants, tucked into her hateful boots, and all topped off with a broad-brimmed hat. All she needed was a shovel and someone might mistake her for a ditch-digger. Good thing she had no intention of seducing Jay today — the only sexy thing she could do in these mundane clothes was a striptease as she took them off. Something she'd never stoop to. What if someone saw?

To her surprise, Jay was already waiting for her, wearing shorts, a polo shirt and — she glanced down — a well-worn pair of boots. So the rock star did own shoes after all.

"Boat's not here yet," he said, jerking his head toward

the jetty.

Gaia smiled. "We're not taking a boat. We'll be flying." As if to punctuate her point, the sound of an approaching helicopter thumped in the distance.

They both watched the aircraft circle overhead before settling down behind a screen of palm trees.

"Come on." Gaia set off toward the helipad. After a moment, she heard Jay scuffing along behind her.

The pilot held the door open for her, so she climbed in before beckoning to Jay, who stood beside the gate with a mulish look on his face. "What are you waiting for?" she demanded.

"Yeah…I don't like helicopters much at the moment. Not after the last one I was in crashed."

Gaia tutted. "You have nothing to worry about this time. I've secured the best helicopter pilot in Western Australia, I'm told."

"It wouldn't have crashed if you hadn't decided to jump out of it while it was in the air," Shou growled.

The rock star jumped out of a flying helicopter? He was more of a thrill seeker than she'd thought.

"I wouldn't have had to if you hadn't tried to – "

"Boys!" Gaia interrupted. "This is my expedition. You – " she pointed at Shou " – are contracted to fly me and my guests wherever I ask you to. And you wanted to see Lorikeet Island, which means no jumping out early, right?"

Jay snorted. Gaia waited, but it seemed to be all the response she was going to get.

"Well then. Let's get going." She settled in her seat as Jay rounded the cockpit to the door on the other side.

Jay climbed in.

"And one other thing," the pilot said, eyeing Gaia, then Jay. "There will be absolutely no sex in my helicopter. You got that?"

Jay laughed. "Sure thing, mate. I'm not sleeping with her. When Flavia gets back, though…you better keep your bird in the air, because if she wants another round in here, I'm not going to refuse. That girl takes her membership in the Mile High Club very seriously."

Gaia hid a smile. If she had any say in it, the rock star's cheap tart wouldn't be coming back to the island any time soon. In fact, she'd go into hiding for a long, long time.

"I bet you've never had sex in the air."

Gaia turned to find Jay's eyes on her as a blush crept across her cheeks. "Of course not."

"I'm sure Shou would be willing to fix that for you. I mean, I might've broken his baby in for him, but I bet he's dying to try it out for himself. You two could fly off into the sunset, engage the autopilot and…maybe he'll let you hold his stick for a bit." Jay laughed at her discomfort.

"For your information, I don't have sex with every man I meet. Unlike some people," Gaia snapped.

Jay stretched, his fingers brushing the ceiling. "I don't know who you mean. Can't be me. I mean, I can't recall the last time I had sex with a man. How about you, Shou? Something about you Xan should know?"

The pilot pressed his lips together, but didn't respond.

Gaia focussed on trading her hat for her headset without mussing her hair too much. When she saw Jay had donned his headset, she whipped out her phone and held it out for a selfie. "Smile for the company magazine," she said, forcing herself to follow her own order as she snapped a few pictures.

She was surprised to find Jay had grinned through every shot. At least the man had decent media training.

Tucking her phone away, she addressed the pilot: "Can we go over the itinerary for today?"

He levelled off, so the entire Buccaneer Archipelago spread out before them, before he replied, "Sure. Flyover of Lorikeet Island and Yampi Sound, before landing on our temporary helipad. Baz took it out by boat this morning. His fee – a couple cases of beer – will be billed to you at the resort. After landing, you'll be free to explore the island. Lunch is already aboard, thanks to the resort's catering department, and depending on our schedule, you can have it at Lorikeet or Baz has offered the jet boat to access some of the sand cays as part of your afternoon charter."

Gaia nodded in approval, then realised the pilot couldn't see her. "And we'll arrive at Lorikeet Island…?"

"Right now on our right. I'll do a high flyover first, then approach from the east, like a plane would for landing, and fly low over the island in a couple of passes to give you a better look before we land. Baz picked a spot on the road for a landing pad, he said, but I'm not sure how close it is to the camp, or even what state the rest of the road's in. Here we go."

Gaia leaned in toward Jay, pointing out the window. "That's the port, where the ships come in to collect our iron ore." The rust coloured piers, topped by a conveyor, stood out in strange contrast to the turquoise sea. Maybe it was because the sea wall was missing and the tide appeared to be in, licking at the island with every wave. Yet the island didn't look as bleak as the first time she'd seen it, only two days ago. Was it the company, or just the absence of threatening clouds? Gaia wasn't sure.

She swallowed painfully. "The mine was there, where that deep water is now." If she stared at it hard enough, maybe she could will the wall back into being.

"I know," Jay said. "I told you, I can see the mine from the highest point on Romance Island. I've watched the trucks creeping down the incline, smaller than the toys I used to play with in the sandpit as a kid. I wouldn't mind taking one of those full-sized Haulpaks for a spin."

"You can't. We only employ female drivers." Gaia almost laughed at the surprise on Jay's face. "What, you thought only men worked at Lorikeet Island? We learned early on that women are better drivers. Fewer accidents means less down time and fewer injuries. It's more efficient that way."

"There weren't any women in the evacuation boats, " Jay said. "Not that I saw, anyway. Maybe if they were really butch, I might not have noticed them, though."

"The last shift of drivers didn't make it to the island before the evacuation order came. They're first to leave and last to arrive, always. I thought it was because it took some time for the miners to extract a full truckload of ore, but it's safety. Some of the guys out there…they're men who don't get along well with other people. Men who don't have many qualifications or skills, and a surprisingly large percentage of them have done time in prison. Car thieves, backyard drug dealers and violent criminals, for the most part, and some of them…aren't safe around women. Aren't safe around most people, to be honest, which is why the mine site's completely dry. No alcohol whatsoever. Anyway, the drivers have their own accommodation block, up near the garage. You can't even see it now — it backed onto the cliffs below the airstrip. Most of that was buried in the landslide when the rain loosened up the airstrip and it slid down the hill. Hard to believe there was a cliff there, higher than the one where my grandfather first started mining." Gaia's pointing finger drifted from the muddy slope to the terraced cliffs above the port. "We'll have to bring in more mining equipment to dig out the trucks. The equipment sheds are under water now, along with everything in them."

"Where's the mining camp?" Jay asked, leaning over her to peer out the window.

Gaia felt unusually hot, with him so close, but she tried to hide the tremor in her voice as she replied, "Down there, under the mud. There's nowhere for them to stay, which is why I need your resort."

Jay grunted and shifted back to his seat. He surveyed the island for a moment, before he said, "So, what are those buildings?"

"Those old Queenslanders?" Gaia dismissed the fibro homes, raised on stilts like the old colonial buildings in Broome. "Full of asbestos. Why the storm couldn't have buried those instead of the newer buildings, I don't know. They were built during World War II when there was a secret army base out here. They camouflaged them to keep the Japanese planes from spotting them, I'm told. Instead of being torn down, they were refitted to be part of the resort, back in the eighties, but nobody uses them now. And some idiot in town got them heritage listed with the local council, so now we can't touch them. Maybe if I'm lucky, they'll collapse in the next storm."

"Not likely, if they've stood there for seventy years. They built to last back then."

Gaia sniffed. "Built to kill, more like. That's how my grandfather died. Asbestosis destroyed his lungs. He never got to retire out here like he'd planned." The helicopter rose over the ridge and communications tower that marked the highest point of the island. The ridge narrowed into a low-lying peninsula, bracketed by two spectacular beaches, which ended in another rise of rock. This was topped by her grandfather's private villa, overlooking the ocean. "You can see the whales from there."

Jay peered out the window. "I don't see any."

"They're only here half the year, I think. I don't know. My grandfather's villa houses some whale researchers when the whales come up. They observe them and count them and…whatever else it is researchers do." She drew herself up proudly. "As long as the mine remains open, we can support projects like whale research. Yampi Sound is unique. We have the largest population of humpback whales in the world – more than thirty thousand, the latest reports say – and they all come up here to breed, every year." There. Chew on that, Jay Felix. Protesters would be beating down his door if he forced her to cut the budget on whale research.

"Yeah, I know. I've watched them humping from my house. Bet your grandfather pulled chicks really easily, too. I mean, he wouldn't have to ask girls back to his house for coffee or to see his etchings. They could come out here to watch whales humping to really get them in the mood."

Gaia's cheeks heated. "I'm sure he did nothing of the sort."

Jay laughed. "Your mother had to come from somewhere. From what I hear, he wasn't exactly young when she was born, either. He had to throw a sweetener in there somehow." He leaned in. "Go on, tell me the thought of whales doing it in the water doesn't make you hot."

Gaia crossed her legs self-consciously. How on earth did he know?

"Are you ready to land, or do you want me to do another sweep?" Shou asked, his interruption so welcome Gaia almost wanted to kiss the pilot.

"Yes, land, please." On the ground, she could put some space between her and Jay so he couldn't see the effect he had on her. She had to think like the businesswoman she was, not some horny teenager who just wanted to rip Jay's clothes off and…

"So I can go for a walk and leave you lovebirds to it, hey?" Jay said.

Gaia wanted to smack the smile off his smug face. "No. So I can get out of this helicopter and away from you."

"So no island tour any more? You reneging on our deal?"

"No." She sucked in a breath. "I'll still take you on the tour. I just need some air, is all. And space."

Jay shrugged. "Whatever, baby. I know I make everyone hot. Even you. Nothing to be ashamed of."

The pilot snorted, then banked in a tight turn as he came in to land.

Gaia forced her breathing to stay even. She couldn't afford to lose control while she was alone with Jay. Her cool, calm business head had to prevail, while her hormones took a hike. At least, until she'd finished with

Flavia.

NINETEEN

The pilot opened her door and Gaia climbed out, her boots crunching on the rocky, red dirt as she stepped off the helipad matting. She stood on the road between the beach and camp, staring at the deep ditch in the sand where someone had dragged the rolled-up matting from the water to its current position. It looked frighteningly like the crocodile tracks she'd been shown in her safety briefings when she'd first joined the company. She glanced around, worried.

Jay was taking his sweet time getting out, and he'd probably only laugh at her fears, so she turned to the pilot. Pointing at the tracks, she asked, "Are there any crocodiles out here?"

The pilot's smile was gentle, without a hint of laughter. "On the mainland, yes, and some of the nearer islands, but I've never heard stories about them swimming this far out to sea. You can see from the footprints on either side that it was Baz, not a croc." He stamped his foot, then pointed at the print he left behind. "See the ridges? Those ones are smooth. Crocs have claws and they don't wear reef sandals. The rest of us are wearing boots. Those are Baz prints from this morning."

She relaxed a little, until the pilot's words had sank in. The only footprints on the island belonged to the three of them, and the mysterious Baz. The cyclone had wiped away all traces of the miners and they were too far out to sea for crocodiles to swim. Suddenly, a field trip to this remote island didn't seem like the wisest plan. The cliffs rose up, hemming her in, as the wind whipped up a willy-willy in the dust at the top of the hill. Her mouth grew dry as the whirling dust. What if something happened to her? Or the pilot? How would they get back if he got hurt and couldn't fly? Or the helicopter was damaged in another landslide? Or...

"Baz'll be here in a couple of hours with the boat, just like you asked. You can check his shoes then, if you like," the pilot reassured her.

As if she cared about the man's shoes. But a boat...she breathed again. A boat was another way off the island if something bad happened. She could manage a couple of hours out here until the boat arrived. Her business depended on it.

Gaia pulled her phone out and passed it to the pilot. "Could you please take some pictures while we're walking around the island? Like we discussed on the phone when we agreed on the itinerary." She avoided his eyes, but she saw him nod as he took the phone from her. He knew what she needed. Now it was her job to make sure he got it.

She set off up the road toward what remained of the mining camp. "You coming?" she called over her shoulder at the two men.

Grunts and the crunch of footsteps followed her, so she trudged on.

TWENTY

By halfway up the final hill, Gaia was so breathless she could barely speak. Hadn't she spent enough time in her private gym lately? Was that why she was so unfit? Or was it the heat and the dust combined that made the steep slope such a challenge?

She glanced at Jay, who powered past her with a grin on his face. "C'mon, slowpoke. You want to see what's at the top, don't you?"

Her grandfather's villa, now the whale observatory.

"I need to catch my breath," she wheezed.

"C'mon." Jay stretched out his hand.

Gaia glanced back, satisfied to see the pilot raising her phone to photograph them. She grasped Jay's hand and trudged up to his side. He'd continued on, so she clung tighter to his fingers as with each panting breath she climbed higher up to the peak of this bloody rock. What on earth had her grandfather liked about the place? It was desolate and dry, full of bright colours that hurt her eyes, all baked in cloying heat that stole her breath. Maybe the old man had been mad to build out here. Her mother had never said so, but she'd also never wanted to visit the place. Hence why she'd given up his house to the whale watchers. That and because it was a tax break, investing in research like this. It also let her claim the cost of maintaining the compound as a tax deduction.

Sweat ran into her eyes. When Gaia tried to wipe it away, her hand came away rusty, as if the moisture had magically attracted more dust to cling to her face. Great. Good thing she wasn't trying to seduce Jay today. She must look a right mess.

"Come on!" Jay yanked on her arm as he ran up the last bit of the slope, almost pulling her over.

Gaia caught her balance just in time to stop herself from falling flat on her face, then took a few more steps to see what had Jay transfixed.

He whistled. "This view's better than the one from my place."

Gaia stepped up to his side and stared at the spectacular view. The whole of Yampi Sound spread out before them, devoid of whales but full of plenty other marine life.

"Big pod of dolphins over there," Jay said.

Gaia couldn't see anything resembling a dolphin. "Where?"

Jay's arm curled around her waist, sending her heart skipping, as he pointed with his free arm. "Right...there."

Gaia saw the splash and squinted into the distance. It looked like something jumped out of the water, then landed with an even bigger splash.

"We have a dolphin protection program, too, you know," she said. "It was one of the initiatives we offered to fund when we constructed the port. The dolphins here are found nowhere else in the world and they're on the endangered list. Without our protection, they'd die out."

"Seems to me, your port's the only thing out here they need protection from," Jay remarked.

"Of course it's not," Gaia snapped, stung. "If it weren't for us, there wouldn't be any fish for them to eat. The port protects them. Fishermen aren't allowed to fish in our shipping lanes. If they were, they'd catch everything in sight and leave nothing for the dolphins."

"Bullshit. Even I know the fishing laws in WA won't allow that to happen. It's why our fish is more expensive than any of the stuff we import, but it's worth it. Knowing you pulled your barramundi or groper out of local waters instead of some sewage farm in South Korea or Thailand."

Gaia didn't know a thing about fishing. Her mother had never allowed her to do such a thing. "What do you mean?"

"It's the foreign fish you have to watch out for," Jay replied patiently. "Cheap barra comes from overseas fish farms, and you need to check to make sure if it's Aussie or not. And if it's wild caught, it could be illegal. We've had the local Fisheries boats come out to the island, chasing illegal fishing boats, and they stop for a drink if they have time. To hear them tell it, illegal immigrants aren't the only thing Indonesian fishing boats come to Australia for. Now they come to steal fish. They sneak into Aussie waters, use nets and fish attraction devices and dynamite and all sorts of shit that's illegal here, fill up their boat with their stolen catch, and sail home. If the Fisheries boys don't catch them first. When they do catch them, they have themselves a big bonfire, burning the fishing boats so they can't come back."

She hadn't heard about illegal fishing before, but it made sense. "See? If we weren't out here, those illegal fishing boats might never get caught, because there'd be no one out here to catch them."

Jay grunted in what she hoped was agreement, then strode off down the track.

Hurrying to catch up with him, Gaia repeated all the things she'd memorised the night before when she'd planned this trip. She talked about the remediation and revegetation programs Vasse Prospecting paid for throughout the islands; the expeditions they'd funded to find and destroy unexploded ordinance from all the target practice during the war and afterwards; the apprenticeship program they funded in town to train local youth to take up positions in the mining industry; the similar program they ran in the men's prison in the Pilbara; the jobs they provided for local people and unskilled labourers; the bird sanctuary on Lorikeet Island…and that was just off the top of her head. Jay fell silent, impressed by her company's social and environmental reputation, or at least she hoped so.

She didn't pause for breath until they reached the helicopter again, after touring the entire perimeter of what remained of the mining camp.

"So, what do you think? I bet you didn't know half of what Vasse Prospecting does for the community. In fact, I'm sure you thought all we did was mining!" A nervous giggle escaped, which Gaia was quick to silence.

Jay shrugged. "I'm hungry. When's lunch?"

Lunch? Surely it wasn't anywhere near noon yet. Gaia glanced at her watch. She was surprised to discover that it was just after one in the afternoon – they'd been talking and hiking around the island for more than two hours. No wonder she was thirsty.

The pilot produced a foam cooler box.

"Thank fuck! I hope you have cold drinks in that." Jay ripped the lid off the box. His face lit up as he fished out a beer and cracked it open. He downed half the can in one gulp, then wiped his mouth with the back of his hand, sighing in pleasure, looking for all the world like a blue-collar worker in a beer commercial.

Gaia felt a jolt in her midsection. For the first time in her life, she wanted to drink beer, licking it off Jay's lips and fingers before kissing him, the taste of his cold tongue in her mouth, coated in the dry drink, as his hands caressed her, undressed her, and –

Jay thrust something cold into her hand. "Fuck, take it. You looked like you were about to jump me for mine. If I'd known how much you love beer, I'd have said ladies first."

Gaia gazed at the beer can he'd given her. It wasn't what she wanted, but she'd have to drink it now, or admit to her fantasy about him. He'd only laugh and reject her again.

She slid a finger under the ring pull, jerking the can open, before taking a slow sip. Ugh, it tasted awful, but at least it was cold. She sucked at the can a little longer, trying not to gag at the taste. How something so cold and wet could be as dry as sandpaper on her tongue, she didn't understand.

Jay crunched his empty can in one hand and flung it into

the rubbish bin in the helicopter cabin. "What's for lunch?"

The pilot pulled out a folding table and proceeded to set it up on the beach, complete with tablecloth and cutlery. This time it was Jay who led the way, sliding into a seat before Gaia sank into hers.

"You not joining us?" Jay asked the pilot.

"Nah, my lunch is up there." He nodded at the helicopter.

Jay shrugged and served himself, too caught up in his quest for food to notice the pilot taking pictures of the two of them. Gaia's smile grew. She selected some sort of sandwich and sank her teeth into it, not really tasting the filling. Her mouth tasted of dust and beer, anyway — anything was an improvement over that.

Despite the dust and drinks, though, her day was definitely going according to plan. Now if only Jay would continue to cooperate this afternoon.

TWENTY-ONE

The talk turned from turtle sanctuaries to ancient rock art to dolphins as the jet boat skimmed over the waves and between the whirlpools skirting the uninhabited islands. Sleek bodies surfed their bow wave before leaping off in search of food. Gaia had never seen so many dolphins in her life and she had to admit, she now saw why people were so passionate about protecting them. They looked like they were smiling and happy and having fun all the time, as if they didn't have a care in the world.

Jay wore a similar expression, whooping when the boat sped up or he spotted something else he wanted to point out. A thrill seeker, through and through. He was like a hyperactive child, but one who set her heart racing and the rest of her body reacting in the most unprofessional way.

Gaia had long since lost count of the number of times she'd told herself she wanted the man's island, not his body, but right now, with the taste of salt on her lips and Jay sitting next to her in a soaking wet shirt from the last wave that had splashed the boat, she was seriously contemplating climbing into his lap. She blamed the beer. She should never have had the second one with her lunch.

Now her belly was roiling and she wasn't sure if it was desire or seasickness. Probably the latter. That might explain her strange fever.

The jet boat slowed to a stop in a rocky bay. To her surprise, Gaia recognised the pilot standing on the beach. He still held her phone. Good.

"I can't go in any closer, or I'll get bogged," Baz said. "The water's pretty shallow here. Barely knee deep. You'll be fine walking back to shore."

Jay nodded, leaping over the side of the boat without a qualm. Sure enough, the water barely reached to his knees. His tied-together boots dangled from one hand. "You coming, baby?"

Gaia peered over the side. She spotted a shell-lined hole like the one she'd lost her shoe to on Romance Island. Only this one was much bigger. She wondered how much bigger the crab was, and shuddered. "No, I...I don't want to get my shoes wet again."

Jay snorted. "So take 'em off. I did."

And let the crabs have her bare toes? "Oh, no." She drew herself up. "You'll have to take me up to the shore. All the way in the boat."

Baz's half lidded eyes regarded her. "Sure. In six hours when the tide's high enough."

Six hours? She couldn't stay out here that long. She had to get back to the resort.

"You big baby. C'mon, princess." Jay scooped her up and lifted her out of the boat, boots and all.

Gaia squealed in surprise, wrapping her arms around his neck. After a moment, she realised that he didn't intend to drop her, so she loosened her hold and settled against his hard chest. This wasn't so bad. At least he hadn't turned caveman and thrown her over his shoulder again. Now, he carried her like his new bride.

He splashed through the shallow water to the beach before he set her on her feet. "I'm not waiting six hours for you to whine about getting your feet wet. I'll miss the *Simpsons*."

A grown man who still watched cartoons? It figured. Gaia glanced at the pilot, who lowered her phone and gave her a barely perceptible nod. He'd captured the whole thing on camera. Good. The day had worked out better than she'd expected.

TWENTY-TWO

Gaia waited until she was certain Jay's attention was fixed on something outside the helicopter windows before she pulled out her phone on the flight home. Even on the small screen, she could see the photos the pilot had taken were exactly what she'd hoped for. If her mother had been alive, Gaia would have received a lecture on being too friendly with her business competitors, but as far as she was concerned, she hadn't been quite friendly enough. That would change. She'd make sure of that.

She directed her phone to upload the pictures to her file sharing service. There might not be any mobile phone reception between Lorikeet and Romance Island, but they'd send as soon as the phone connected to a network. Stephanie would know exactly what to do with them.

As she tucked her phone away again, she glanced at Jay, who still stared out the window. Perfect. He hadn't noticed a thing.

Idly, she wondered if she should ask Jay to dinner tonight, or whether that would mess with her plans too much. What was wrong with her? She couldn't seem to stay away from the man. Everything about him drew her toward him, even as her mind screamed at her that he was rude and annoying and irritating and maddening and…Jay Felix, the perfect male specimen she'd lusted after all through university. Her mother wouldn't have let her near him, but Morrigan wasn't here to stop her any more.

Gaia's life and the company were in her own hands now.

She grimaced. For the good of the company, she should avoid him until tomorrow. Let him have time to think over his decision while other pieces moved into play. Too soon and she'd spoil everything.

Maybe she should invest in a marital aid. Something to keep her mind off the complete lack of available men on the badly named Romance Island. Ugh. But not yet. Only if she failed would she need one of those battery operated…things. She suppressed a shudder and sat up straighter.

Things could still turn out in her favour. Fortune favoured her, like it favoured her whole family. She couldn't possibly fail.

TWENTY-THREE

The landing was rough enough to jolt Gaia out of her doze. She couldn't have fallen asleep, surely. She smoothed her clothes as the pilot walked around to her door and opened it for her.

Gaia hopped out, or at least she tried to. Instead, her stiff legs and heavy boots almost made her fall over as she crashed to the ground. The pilot caught her and she allowed him to keep holding her until she was certain she was steady on her feet. A quick glance back told her Jay hadn't seen her clumsiness — he was busy clambering out the other side.

She shook off the pilot and hadn't made it two steps before she heard him say, "Do you need me tomorrow, ma'am?"

Gaia pursed her lips. She had to do something to distract herself during the day. "Maybe. I'll let you know in the morning."

The pilot nodded and climbed back into his aircraft.

Not wanting to be nearby when he took off, Gaia hurried off the helipad, only to find Jay blocking the path to the villas.

"Do you want your answer now?" he drawled.

She deliberately delayed, letting her gaze rake down his body. Even in his salt-encrusted clothes, he still looked like sex on a stick. She had no illusions about her own appearance, though – her pressed shirt was now horribly creased, and the thought of the dried salt on her skin from seawater and sweat made her itch. Not to mention the dust that had gotten everywhere. She wanted a shower.

"I think we should both go clean up, have a rest and sleep on it. Tomorrow, let's meet for dinner to discuss my proposal."

He shrugged, then slouched off.

Gaia stared after him, not sure whether to call him back or call him a rude bastard.

"So that's a yes, then?" she called after him.

She wasn't certain, but she thought he gave her another shrug before he disappeared into the darkness.

TWENTY-FOUR

Gaia scrubbed her skin in the shower, but nothing she did seemed to make her feel fresh again. Plus, her feet hurt from being stuck in those awful boots all day. She needed a proper pedicure, or she wouldn't want to walk another step tomorrow.

She towelled herself dry and picked up the phone. "Get me the resort day spa," she instructed.

"I'm sorry, ma'am, but the day spa isn't open right now," the flustered receptionist replied.

Gaia gritted her teeth. "Then when will they be open? I need the earliest possible appointment."

A nervous cough. "Not until June, ma'am."

"Nine? Fine. Book me in for their best pedicure and make sure it includes a thorough foot massage."

The girl tittered. "I said June, ma'am, not nine o'clock. As in, the day spa isn't open until peak season."

Anger charged Gaia's veins. "June? But that's weeks away. I simply cannot wait. Find me a beautician who can do a pedicure by nine tomorrow morning." She hung up.

After Gaia had dressed, ordered some room service and chosen a suitable movie for the evening, the phone rang.

"Yes?"

"As requested, I booked you an appointment at one of the spas in Cable Beach. They were the only ones with a vacancy tomorrow morning." The receptionist hesitated. "Would you like me to arrange transport for you, too, ma'am?"

Why hadn't she done it already? "Yes."

"Helicopter or jet boat and charter plane, ma'am?"

"The helicopter, of course," Gaia snapped.

"Very good, ma'am. Will there be anything else?"

There wasn't, but Gaia decided to invent things, anyway. "Arrange for a catered lunch for me tomorrow at the best restaurant in town. I don't care where, just make sure they have the best and the freshest Broome has to offer." Another thought occurred to her. "Oh, and I'd like a private dinner for two for tomorrow evening at seven. Tell the chef I want it romantic, private and of the highest standard. With two bottles of your best champagne. No, make it three." She'd definitely want to toast her triumph when Jay gave in to her.

Over the island, of course.

Winning him over in a romantic sense would be a piece of cake, what with the plan she had in place.

TWENTY-FIVE

"My feet have soaked quite long enough," Gaia told the girl irritably.

The spa attendant produced a serene smile. "A few more minutes, madame. You are here for a Polynesian foot spa, and the oils take time to penetrate your skin. This treatment isn't just about your feet. With the aromatherapy oils, you should experience total relaxation, which cannot be rushed. I promise you, this is like no other pedicure you have ever experienced before."

It certainly took longer than any other she'd experienced before. She hadn't even seen the colour chart yet.

Finally, the girl towelled her feet dry and began to massage Gaia's toes. Perhaps this wasn't so bad, Gaia decided, closing her eyes as she relaxed in her seat.

At some point, another girl appeared, carrying a tiny cup of herbal tea and the varnish colours. Gaia had picked her colours before the cup reached her lips. A French manicure in neutral colours with a slightly pearlescent sheen. Anything more garish would make her look like one of the common women who were nothing like her. She vividly recalled the one time she and Helen had painted their fingernails purple on the way home from school, only for her mother to summon her personal beautician to remove the offending colour, making Gaia promise never to cheapen herself in such a way again.

Just as the first butterfly-soft strokes of the undercoat touched her toes, Gaia's phone rang.

The girl kneeling at her feet frowned. "No phones in the spa, madame, for it will ruin the relaxation experience. I must ask you to – "

Gaia ignored her. "Hello?"

"Miss Vasse, it's Stephanie. I received the files you sent yesterday and forwarded them to my contacts with a modified press release. Are you sure you want this to replace the announcements about the new mine?"

"Of course I do. I said so, didn't I?" Gaia snapped.

"It's just that we've been preparing the campaign for the new uranium mine for months now, and if we give the evening news spot to this media release, one of the other channels might pick up the mine opening in a less favourable light before we've had a chance to solidify our approach in the hearts and minds of – "

Gaia's breath hissed out angrily. "I don't care about the uranium mine, or what the public has to say about it. The mine can wait a week or even a month if it has to. This is essential to my negotiations today. We have far more invested in Lorikeet Island than we'll ever have in a uranium mine that's barely a hole in the ground right now."

"Yes, Miss Vasse." A pause. "Oh, and there's another matter. The editor of their women's magazine wants to run a celebrity gossip piece with the pictures you sent. A follow up to tonight's TV spot. Would you like me to issue a statement refuting the rumours, or allow them to stand?"

A gossip magazine wanted to show the world the pictures of her and Jay? Gaia rubbed her hands together in glee. Her mother had bought shares in the international media company because she'd wanted control over what they printed. Morrigan hadn't understood that the media didn't work that way – the papers printed what they wanted, unfounded or not. The trick was to give them exactly the sort of thing they wanted to print, while spinning it in such a way that they couldn't help but take your side in controversial matters. What the gossip magazines wanted was a trusted source who gave them more than they could invent on their own.

"Neither. Tell the editor, off the record, that the rumours are true." By the time the story went to print, they would be. "Say it's been kept secret for a while, because of my mother's ill health, but now it's time to reveal the truth or whatever it is you say."

"Yes, Miss Vasse." Stephanie's nails ticked on a computer keyboard. "The report I sent last night has just hit the morning news programmes. It looks like another media frenzy, bigger than the first. Would you like me to send you the links?"

"Forward them to my email. I'll look at them if I have a chance," Gaia replied. She didn't care what the media said, unless it reflected badly on her or her company. "Anything I should be concerned about yet?"

"Definitely not. I sent the report anonymously; there's nothing that can link it to us. I was just a concerned and unusually observant citizen who accidentally came into possession of some compromising emails sent from a computer in an internet café..."

Gaia smiled. She knew there was nothing accidental about her media manager's ability to acquire access to email accounts that weren't hers. That's why she kept the woman onside as much as possible. There was so much Mother hadn't understood about public perception and media management, but Gaia hadn't done a double degree, majoring in both media and business, for nothing. Mother had been too old fashioned in so much of what she did, believing her father's way to be the only way to do business. And Grandfather had been conservative at heart, a legacy he'd definitely passed on to his daughter.

But Gaia did things differently, and there was no one to hold her back now. This was her time.

Gaia glanced at her boring toenails, as the girl brushed the last two with pale pink polish. Conservative. Boring. Time for a change.

"I don't like the colour," Gaia declared. She fished through the colour charts and found the one she wanted. "It should be this one." She squinted at the name. "Feeding frenzy red."

"But, madame, I am almost finished. You asked for – "

Gaia interrupted, "I've changed my mind. I want this one instead. And on my fingernails, too."

Purple might have looked tawdry on her teenage self, but Gaia knew nothing the chairman of Vasse Prospecting wore would ever appear cheap. Her blood-dipped talons couldn't wait to get stuck into Jay Felix and his island. Romance Island Resort would soon be hers. Along with the romance she craved.

TWENTY-SIX

By the time Gaia climbed into the helicopter for the flight back to Romance Island that afternoon, she felt much more herself. Her pedicured feet were no longer a source of shame; the day spa had talked her into a body wrap to bring out the best in her skin; and a hair appointment had dealt with the damage from yesterday's field trip. If it weren't for the red dust and boabs in town, she'd almost think she was in civilisation again.

Soon. Once she'd negotiated everything she wanted from Jay Felix.

Gaia stopped at the resort's business centre to print out the contract documents she'd asked the Vasse Prospecting legal department to assemble for her. If she and Jay reached an agreement tonight, she wanted to have all the paperwork on hand to sign right away, before he changed his mind.

She placed the pile of papers carefully on the dining

table, garnishing it with a hotel-issue pen. She wouldn't be caught unprepared.

Tonight was definitely about business.

Instead of white, this time she chose a black dress, matching her nails with a glossy lipstick she'd bought from the range at the day spa. She reached for a pair of heels, then reconsidered and picked a pair of strappy sandals instead. Slightly more suitable for a romantic walk on the beach, if she chose to invite Jay for one later.

At precisely seven, her door chimed.

"Who is it?" she sang out.

"Catering, ma'am," came the reply. "Your private dining room is ready for you. Romantic, as requested."

Gaia palmed open the door. "Show me," she commanded.

The waiter bowed before gesturing toward the path to her private beach. "This way, ma'am."

She followed the man to the beach, where she found a white-skirted table set for two. But her date was nowhere to be seen.

"Where is Jay Felix?" she asked.

The waiter shrugged. "I believe he's at home, ma'am. I can call Reception to check for you."

Gaia waved him away. "Don't bother. I'll find him myself."

He wasn't going to keep her waiting for this dinner. Even if she had to drag him all the way from his house to the table.

She held her head high as she marched to Villa Penguin. When she reached the veranda, she rapped sharply on the door, but no one answered. Had the man forgotten their meeting again? She pressed her ear to the door, hoping to hear some movement inside. To her surprise, she heard his voice, speaking low and fast, though she couldn't discern the words.

"It's all over the six o'clock news! They hounded me at home and at work and my own boss called me a whore before she fired me!" a female voice shrieked tinnily, as if through television speakers.

"Flavia, baby, please. I swear – " Jay began.

Or on the phone, Gaia thought with satisfaction.

"You're a lying, cheating sack of shit, you arsehole. I saw you with that other girl. She has more money than me, and I meant nothing to you, because you were after her all along! At least James paid for his prostitute – did you pay her, or did she pay you? You know what? I don't care. You're a selfish, cheating bastard, and I never want to see you again!" the harpy continued.

"Baby, wait…WAIT!" Beeping and swearing, then the sound of something smashing against the floor. "Fuck!"

His little tart was his no longer. Gaia grinned.

The door flew open, and she found herself face to face with an anguished rock star wearing a shirt and shorts, but no shoes. "What are you doing here? Get out of my way," he growled, pushing past her.

"Our dinner engagement," she reminded him. "We agreed to a dinner meeting to discuss my proposal about the island."

"Not interested. Unless you have bourbon." He eyed her balefully.

He wanted to get drunk? Gaia panicked for a moment, before calm washed over her. Negotiating with inebriated businessmen was easier than sober ones. Perhaps she could get a better price for the island if she waited until he was drunk, or close to it.

"I'm sure the waiter can provide whatever you'd like to drink. I understand the resort has a well-stocked bar," Gaia said.

"Fine."

Gaia linked her arm with his, but he shook her off. She shrugged and said instead, "This way. I asked for a romantic dinner, so your staff set up a table on my private beach."

"Fucking awesome." He stomped off, but he did head in the direction of the beach.

Gaia followed, picking her way carefully to make sure no crab tried to steal her shoes this time.

When Jay reached the table, he stopped dead. "This is the worst fucking joke I've seen all year. How did you know?"

"Know what?" she asked.

He waved at the table. "This. All this. I romanced Flavia with a dinner on the beach. All candles and flowers and shit."

"I had no idea," she admitted truthfully. "How about you sit down and tell me all about it?"

"Why the fuck should I talk to you?"

She shrugged. "I'm a willing ear and I'm here. You're evidently upset about something. I thought you might like to talk about it. Unless you wish to discuss business, like we're supposed to. I'm amenable to that, too."

"Amenable. What kind of fucking word is amenable?"

She coughed to cover a laugh. "It means — "

"I know what it fucking means. I'm not an idiot, even if

I am an arsehole, according to some." Jay glared at her. "I don't want amenable. I want bourbon. A lot of it."

A waiter who must have been hiding just out of sight cleared his throat as he approached them. "Can you get you anything to drink? Champagne, perhaps?" He gestured at the bottle in the ice bucket.

"Yes," Gaia said at the same time as Jay snapped, "Bourbon. And bring the whole bottle."

The waiter popped open the champagne and poured her a glass before he trotted off to fulfil Jay's order.

Jay slumped onto his seat, driving the chair legs deep into the sand.

Gaia tucked her skirt carefully as she sat, before lifting her champagne glass. To new beginnings, she toasted silently as she sipped.

TWENTY-SEVEN

Jay swigged from his half-empty bottle of bourbon. "And that's why you should never sleep with a virgin," he finished.

Gaia blinked. That wasn't the conclusion she'd drawn from his tale at all. Leaning across the table, she said, "Maybe it's not because she was a virgin. Maybe it was all about the money."

"Money?" Jay snorted. "She gave it back to me. Didn't take a cent. Said she wanted the sex more."

"And you believed that?"

The bottle slammed down on the table. "Of course I fucking did. I'm awesome in bed. Ask anyone. Even that maid…Audrey…tried to pay her, but she wouldn't take my money. We were perfect together. But she called me names and shit, too. Said I cheated on her." He sighed.

"Did you?" Gaia asked before she could stop herself.

"Sort of," Jay admitted. "She was off doing her weather girl thing and I was being a rock star. Had to sleep with the fans. They expected it. Not that many, though. Only four or five a night."

Gaia's jaw dropped. No man could have sex five times in a night. It wasn't humanly possible. She must have heard wrong. "How many?"

"No more'n five. I only had a six-seater limo, see. We'd get started in the back seat, go back to my hotel room, and once everyone had their turn, we'd go again. Well, some of them. Some of those girls had no stamina. Fell asleep after the first round, when I wanted to go all night." He smirked. "Didn't stop them from asking for more the next morning, though. Once they've had a taste of this rock star, they always want more. I'm just that good."

Gaia felt faint. More than five times in a night, and still up for more in the morning? This man sounded like more than she could handle. Or he was lying. Her eyes narrowed. "Sounds to me like none of those girls were good enough for you."

Jay shrugged. "Good enough for a night, at any rate. They wanted it, I wanted it…that's about it, really. They never forget me and I don't remember them. Yeah. Maybe they just weren't good enough. Not for…me." He tipped the bottle up again.

"Maybe they just wanted to sleep with a rock star. A rich man with your money must be irresistible to girls like that."

Jay eyed her. "I'm irresistible to most women, baby, and a whole lotta men, too."

A blush warmed Gaia's cheeks. He was definitely right about that part.

She cleared her throat. "But what if they only want you for your money? For your fame and what you can do for them? They all want a piece of you, but they've got nothing to offer you in return. Not good enough for you. I bet what you really want is someone who's your equal. Someone who understands what it is to be rich and powerful and wanted."

Jay snorted. "You think I want to fuck some rich bitch? So up herself she doesn't know what the world looks like outside her own arse?"

Gaia shifted uncomfortably. Why did he have to be so coarse? A normal man would apologise. A normal man would realise he'd offended her, that he was wrong about her, and try to make amends.

But she didn't want a normal man. She wanted to prove to Jay Felix that she wasn't the sort of girl he thought she was. She knew how the world worked. People like them shared the power, while the masses lived their insignificant lives not knowing what real power was like.

"Have you ever bedded a billionaire before?" Gaia asked.

"Don't think so. Oh, there was this one chick in Sydney once…a Carwashian or something? Dunno. American chick with fake tits, anyway. They just didn't bounce properly. Nah, she can't have been. Billionaires are kinky. It says so in all the books."

Books about billionaires? Had Jay read that unauthorised biography penned by some old flame of her mother's? Gaia had thought it was all lies, until she'd seen the evidence with her own eyes in her mother's bedside cabinet. Peanut butter, hazelnut spread and a jar of something that looked like whipped marshmallow, and when she'd opened them…every one bore the marks of thick fingers that had dug deep into the gloopy mess. She'd always thought her mother had eaten them while reading in bed as some sort of guilty pleasure, but that trashy book had insisted she liked her lovers to smear the spreads all over her –

"I said, what's your brand of kink?" Jay said loudly, looking annoyed.

Not peanut butter, that's for sure. Gaia moistened her dry mouth. "Why don't you try me and find out?" She downed the last of her champagne, reaching for the bottle to pour more. Huh. Empty. The other bottle was, too. Where was the waiter? She needed another drink. Jay must have drunk all hers while she wasn't looking.

"I'm not drunk enough for that," he said.

A shadow appeared at Gaia's side, tilting a bottle over her glass. She nodded and greedily watched the bubbles rising as her glass filled. She rose unsteadily to her feet, glass in hand. "To getting drunk," she declared.

Jay laughed. "I can drink to that."

Good, Gaia thought, watching him empty the bourbon bottle. Her night wasn't ending without some sort of satisfaction and she knew who she wanted to give it to her.

TWENTY-EIGHT

Gaia stretched, savouring the pleasurable ache between her thighs. She'd waited for too long to scratch that particular itch, but it had been worth the wait. A light slap stung her bare bottom, sending a zing of pleasure straight to her core that melted her insides. "Again," she ordered.

"Nah, baby, I'm going to bed."

Gaia heard the shuffle of footsteps and lay back in drowsy anticipation of Jay joining her again. But the bed didn't move and the sounds died away. "Jay?"

No answer.

She jumped out of bed, only to find her legs didn't want to carry her any more. They seemed to have turned into tentacles or something equally wobbly. "Damn." She collapsed on the mattress again, dreamily remembering all the things Jay had done to her body since they'd finished dinner. No wonder she could barely walk. She'd find him tomorrow, when they could do it all over again.

TWENTY-NINE

Xan answered her phone without looking at the caller. "Xan Lane."

Jay sounded surprisingly alert for such an early hour of the morning. Maybe he hadn't made it to bed yet. "I got the contracts. I only took a quick look, but even I can see it looks like a pretty shit deal for the resort. And there's a bit I really don't like, either. Something about how if the resort isn't making a certain profit margin in any year during the first decade they own it, they can insist on a refund of their purchase price, plus maintenance costs. She wants to stick her mining staff here, so the place won't make a cent in profit. It's basically an agreement to give it to her rent-free for next to nothing for a decade, then get her money back. Or she could sell the place to someone else and make her money back and more." Jay sounded worried. "Look, I don't understand all if it. Lots of legal shit. I've scanned it and I'm sending it through now. She doesn't know I have it, so I'll probably have to get Jackie to sneak it back into her house before she wakes up."

He'd piqued Xan's curiosity. "Don't tell me you slept with her to distract her so you could swipe the paperwork."

"All right, I won't, then."

Silence reigned as Xan digested his words.

"You seduced her? What about Flavia? I thought you and her – "

"We're through. Somehow, the press found out about her. They hounded her at work and home. Someone broke into the place where she works and sprayed stuff on the walls about her. Calling her a whore. She blames me, though I never told anyone, so she said we're over." Jay sounded almost as down as he had after he'd found out about Phuong. Twice unlucky in love. Poor Jay.

"I'm sorry to hear that," Xan said, and meant it. "I liked Flavia."

A heavy sigh. "Yeah, so did I. She doesn't feel the same way any more, though, so I should just get over her and move on. Plenty more fish in the sea."

Not ones who auctioned off their virginity, and they'd be an even rarer breed if Flavia was publicly crucified for doing it.

"Perhaps try a different bait next time," Xan said softly.

"Yeah, well, right now I have this rich chick sniffing around, scaring anyone else off. Have you got everything you need, or do I need to be hospitable to her again?"

Hospitable. Jay sure had a strange definition of hospitality.

"I'll call you if I need anything else, but this contract

should be a good starting point. I'll call their managing director, James Stewart, later on today, to set up a meeting with me and Jo. Maybe we can arrange a reduced rate for rooms in the wet season. Don't worry. We'll take it from here."

Jay seemed satisfied to end the conversation there, so after some hastily-said goodbyes, Xan dialled Vasse Prospecting. James Stewart already owed the resort a favour for helping with their evacuation. This might be a good time to call it in.

THIRTY

Oh God. Make it stop.

But the bright sunlight lanced her scrunched-shut eyelids as some pesky miner hammered incessantly at the inside of Gaia's head. A high-pitched chime stabbed through her eardrums and into her brain.

"Go to hell," she groaned, rolling out of bed. Ow, that only made her head hurt worse.

She staggered to the bathroom for her robe before she dragged her aching body to the door. Who could it possibly be at this ungodly hour?

"Room service," the recorded voice informed her, before the irritating chime sounded again.

She swiped open the door. "I ordered breakfast for ten."

"Yes, ma'am. Romantic breakfast for two at 10 am, as requested. Shall I set the table for you?"

Breakfast for two. Gaia couldn't remember arranging a

breakfast meeting. Wait. Romantic? Was someone else supposed to be here?

Distracted, she waved the waiter in. He wheeled the trolley in and transferred the trays to the table. Flowers. Waffles. Strawberries. Poached eggs. Even the damn bacon. All of it meticulously heart-shaped.

Romantic, all right. And then she remembered. Jay.

Gaia strode to the bedroom, but there was no sign of the man, or that he'd been there at all. Oh, sure, she'd dreamed about him, but that wasn't new. She'd had erotic dreams every night since she arrived at the resort. Only her body didn't usually ache so much after a dream. After a gym workout, maybe. Unless last night she and Jay…

Swallowing, she peered into the bedside bin. On top of the tissues was a collection of used condoms and their brightly coloured wrappers. She counted them both – five and four. No, that couldn't be right. She hooked her foot around the bin and pulled it closer. A ripped red wrapper crackled as the basket moved off it. Five. Five wrappers, five condoms…did she honestly have sex with Jay Felix five times last night? No. No man could manage that. The longest any man lasted in her experience had been twenty minutes, and even that had been a stretch. Certainly not a second time in the same night. It had to be some sort of prank.

Yet she'd confidently ordered breakfast for him, expecting him to join her.

Was it because of the contracts? Hadn't he signed them last night?

Try as she might, Gaia's memories of the previous night were hazy. She knew she'd drunk champagne, matching Jay drink for drink as he downed his bottle of bourbon, but she had no idea how much. More than her hurting head wanted, that was for certain. She hoped she had some headache tablets in here somewhere. She hadn't had a hangover this brutal since…since she could remember, to be honest. She'd always been so careful not to drink too much because drunkenness led to bad judgement and bad judgement was unforgivable in a Vasse.

She pawed through her beauty case until she found a box of pills, then swallowed two with a glass of water. There. That should help her feel better. Now she had to find the contracts, to see whether she was signing or celebrating with Jay this morning.

She ambled back to the dining room, where the waiter still stood.

"Would you like me to open the champagne for you?" he asked.

Champagne? With breakfast? Gaia's stomach issued a gurgled protest. "No."

She scanned the table for the papers she'd left there last night before meeting Jay for dinner. There was no sign of them.

The waiter was almost out the door with his trolley.

"Wait!" she commanded. "Where are the papers that were here?"

"What papers, ma'am?"

Gaia marched him back to the dining room and tapped the table. "Here. I left them right here and now they're gone."

He shrugged. "There was nothing on the table, ma'am. You must have moved them when you heard your breakfast had arrived. Thank you, ma'am."

Of course she hadn't moved them. She'd walked straight from bed to the door. Either he was lying or they'd moved the papers last night.

Gaia scrutinised the shelves of the man's room service trolley, but there was nothing on it but a stack of dish covers. He didn't have her papers. That meant they must be somewhere in the house. Signed, most likely, and placed in a folder with her things, ready to scan when the business centre opened in the morning. Her breath hissed out in relief. "Fine. Go."

The man hurried out, taking his trolley with him.

THIRTY-ONE

Gaia poured herself a cup of tea as black as her mood. She couldn't possibly have forgotten the contracts in order to satisfy her sexual desires, had she? Her mother would be appalled. Stewart would wear that triumphant smile that told her without words that she wasn't fit to run the family firm.

But he was wrong. Stewart could go suck eggs for all she cared. Gaia always put business before pleasure. Always. Her family fortune was far more important than some fling, even with that well-muscled Felix man.

She must have tucked them away somewhere safe.

Gaia managed to swallow exactly two sips of tea before she gave in and started searching. The papers weren't anywhere in the dining room or kitchen. She hadn't tucked them away in a cupboard or drawer. The lounge room wasn't hiding them, and the spare bedroom was as untouched as the day she'd arrived. That left her bedroom and the bathrooms.

A cursory glance told her it wasn't in the main bathroom. Not even in the huge spa tub. Her ensuite, covered in mess from her search for a hangover remedy, didn't have any papers. That left the bedroom.

The bedside tables were empty, and she already knew the bin only held rubbish. The leather portfolio she kept in her carry-on bag, then. Gaia unzipped the soft, fawn-coloured leather and flipped through the pages, but found no contracts. She threw it down on the unmade bed and rifled through her carry-on bag, even opening her laptop to see if it she had mistaken one zip case for another in her tipsiness last night. No, not there, either.

Gaia dumped out the contents of her suitcase and felt every item, including the lining of the bag itself. Nothing. Not a single sheet of paper, let alone a whole contract.

Snarling, she jumped to her feet, her head pounding a warning. To hell with her hangover. She needed that contract.

An hour later, she'd turned the house upside down, moved every stick of furniture and stitch of fabric, only to turn up empty-handed.

Had she taken the papers to Jay's place for him to sign?

No, of course not. If she'd done that, she'd have woken up at his house instead of her own. Unless she'd insisted on having sex in her bed...

Of course. Even after a drink or two, Gaia would never spend the night in a strange man's bed. She'd never stoop so low. Instead, she would have invited him back to her house to provide her with the company she craved. She must have left the signed contract at his house.

She sank onto a dining chair with a sigh of relief, suddenly feeling hungry. Once she'd finished breakfast and freshened up with a shower, she'd take a stroll to Jay's place to pick up her papers.

And then perhaps they could have another private celebration just like last night. Only this time, she intended to remember every moment, instead of just the vague feeling that it had been incredible enough to rival her wildest dreams.

Gaia smiled around her tea cup, her contented sigh sending a waft of steam up toward the ceiling.

THIRTY-TWO

Gaia felt almost human again as she all but skipped along the path to Jay's villa. He hadn't joined her for breakfast, true, but his hangover had to be worse than hers. After all, he'd been drinking straight spirits, not champagne. In a fit of charitableness, she decided to only knock once. If he didn't answer, she'd go for a swim and come back later.

She hadn't even rounded the corner fully before she heard his voice say, "You again."

She found Jay sitting on his veranda, wearing nothing but his wet, clinging board shorts as he crunched into an apple. The man even had perfect teeth, she noticed with heart-swelling approval. She couldn't abide a crooked smile.

"Good morning," she said with a smile.

He shrugged. "What do you want?"

Gaia faltered. He was back to his usual, surly self, as if none of last night had happened. Had he forgotten that they'd spent the night together, enfolded in bliss in her bed? Surely not. She'd make him remember. "I came to thank you for last night," she said.

Another shrug. "It was nothing special."

She tried to hide how much his casual dismissal stung. "And I wanted to ask you whether I left some paperwork here last night. Some contract documents, perhaps?"

He picked up a stack of pages she hadn't noticed sitting on the glass-topped table until now. "You mean these?" He fanned them toward her, his eyes narrowing. "Quite an interesting read."

Now it was her turn to be dismissive. "Hardly. Legal contracts are about as boring as they come. What does it matter? Now they're all signed, we can leave everything for other people to sort out."

Jay flipped through the pages, pulled one out and held it up. "Oh, you mean you actually thought I was going to sign this?"

Gaia peered at the sheet, her heart sinking. There was no signature on it at all. She'd been so distracted by his body and the alcohol in her blood that she'd forgotten to do her job. "It's a standard contract. The legal department drew it up. I haven't really looked at it," she lied.

"That makes two of us," he muttered, flinging the pages back on the table. "I leave this sort of shit to my lawyers."

Gaia breathed a sigh of relief. If he hadn't read it, he couldn't be angry at her. It must be his hangover headache making him so grumpy.

"So why are you still here?" Jay asked, folding his arms across his mesmerising chest.

It took Gaia a moment to drag her eyes up to his face.

"Mmm?"

"I asked you why you're still here."

Nerves fluttered in her tummy. "I was wondering…I was hoping you'd like to join me today. Do something together." Like have incredible sex so she could remember every detail this time.

"Why, so you can try to seduce me into signing shit like this again?" He waved the contract.

Yes. Gaia flushed. Was her desire that obvious?

She summoned her best professional smile, hoping it would give her the confidence to see this through. "After last night, I thought you…I thought you and I…"

"Might want to fuck each other's brains out?" Jay finished for her. "Nah, baby. Once was enough."

No it wasn't, she wanted to cry. Wait – it had been more than once last night. Nobody used up a whole box of condoms for just once.

"But…I'm a billionaire. You said you'd never been to bed with a billionaire before. Once I go home, you might never get another chance. Being with a billionaire is – "

"Boring, baby. You were boring. No better than any other girl and worse than some." Jay didn't even do her the courtesy of looking her in the eye as he trampled on her post-coital bliss. "Maybe it's only billionaire blokes who know what they want, and make things interesting with their particular tastes. Dunno. I don't bang blokes."

Gaia saw red. "How would you know what they're like in bed, then?"

"I read, baby. Maybe you should, too. Read a fucking sex manual, at least. Because sex with you last night…fuck, I have more fun with my own hand."

Gaia turned and fled before he could see her tears. He was lying. He had to be. Five times. They'd done it five times last night and it had been the best night of her life. If only she could remember it better. How dare he call it boring!

She slowed as she reached her own front door, and her scattered thoughts caught up with her. What if he was telling the truth? If he wasn't lying, then five rounds of incredible sex in one night was ordinary for him. How much better would it be if they spent a night together that was so good, even he thought it was extraordinary?

Her core clenched, flooding her lower regions with heat so searing that if she didn't know her knickers were made of silk, she could've sworn they'd melted.

THIRTY-THREE

It took Gaia three days of squirming discomfort before she admitted to herself that she wanted to see Jay again. She'd spent hours watching the resort's adult movie channels, but she was still no wiser about what Jay really wanted. It's not like she could ask him. What if he said he wanted oral sex? She'd watched a dozen different women pleasuring the men in the movies with their mouths, and if she wasn't put off by the idea before that, she was thoroughly disgusted now. All that flesh and fluid and…how did they fit all that in their mouths without choking? What if it tasted awful? Or he hadn't washed? And the hair… Jay wasn't the sort of man to wax it all off, that she already knew. What if she got pubic hair in her teeth? She almost retched at the thought.

It involved getting on her knees, anyway, something she'd never do. Kneeling before a man was beneath her.

No, billionaires did things differently. He'd said

something about knowing what she wanted. Well, she did know. She wanted him. She wanted to see a little more of the spectacular landscape up here, including the rest of the Buccaneer Archipelago, and she wanted more sex with him.

She stood, switched off the TV and summoned the helicopter pilot for a full day's charter. Not a work trip, like the flight to Lorikeet had been. This time she'd be a tourist, seeing the sights the region had to offer.

Gaia made it halfway to Jay's villa before she chickened out. She couldn't stand to see the sneer on his face if he called her boring again, so she turned on her heel and trotted back to her house. Before she could change her mind, Gaia picked up the phone and asked to be transferred to Jay.

The phone rang and rang, but she tightened her grip on the receiver, willing him to answer the call.

She didn't want to do this alone. She craved company like she needed air. Until a few weeks ago, she'd never truly been alone. She'd been surrounded by security or employees and her mother's concerned presence wherever she went. Even when she travelled, Morrigan had called her most nights. But she'd never call her again. Gaia would never hear the gruff voice discussing her day, asking if Gaia was being safe, appropriately aloof, and upholding the family name, then advising her on everything from food to clothing to employee relations. Not even Gaia's brief holiday flings had escaped Morrigan's scrutiny. Her mother had always cautioned her to remain detached, knowing without even meeting the man that he wasn't good enough for her daughter and heiress.

But her mother wasn't here now to make a judgement

on Jay. Would she think he was good enough? He had enough money to make Morrigan pay attention. Money covered a multitude of sins, Morrigan had always said, but once you scratched the surface, you'd see who was common and who was her kind.

What kind was Jay?

"This better be good." His voice on the other end of the phone almost made her drop the receiver.

"Jay! Oh, hello. It's Gaia."

"I knew that. It's on the caller display. What do you want?"

You.

Gaia cleared her throat. "I have a day off to see the sights, and I have a helicopter booked to take me out to see some of the waterfalls."

"Have fun."

No! He couldn't hang up on her!

"Wait! I want you to come with me." Gaia held her breath while she waited for his answer.

She didn't have to wait long.

"Why?"

"Because I don't want to go alone." Even as the words left her lips, she knew they were true.

Jay coughed out a laugh. "You said you have a helicopter. You won't be alone. You'll have the pilot. He's very accommodating to pretty girls, or so I hear."

Her heart leaped in her chest. "Did you just call me pretty?" Gaia demanded.

"Cut the bullshit, baby. If you're going to spend the whole day telling me how saintly you are because your company saves the whales and the rest of the archipelago,

I'm not interested."

She desperately wanted to defend herself. Her company did save things — it said so in their annual report. Right there in the executive summary on the first page. But Jay didn't want to listen. "I'm taking a day off," she said instead. "I don't get many holidays because I'm usually too busy working. I want to see some of the attractions out here before I fly home. The tour brochure said something about the only horizontal waterfalls in the world."

"You're taking a tour? Where you might have to mingle with the public?"

She scowled. "Of course not. It's a private tour. I thought you might like to share it with me. You seem to know the area so much better than I do, seeing as you live here."

"Oh, so you want me as your tour guide now? That'll cost you, baby. I don't come cheap, you know."

She wished she could remember how he came. Had he called her name? Said he loved her? Maybe he'd done both and was embarrassed to admit it. She'd just have to change his mind. Tonight, she promised herself. Getting him drunk worked last time. If she plied him with enough alcohol tonight, he'd surely go to bed with her again.

"But you'll come?" She hated the need she heard in her voice.

"Only if you ask me nicely."

Two could play at that game. "Mr Felix, I would like to extend an invitation for you to accompany me in a private helicopter flight to Horizontal and Mitchell Falls. Refreshments will be provided. Your presence is requested — "

"Fuck, what kind of finishing school forced you to learn that crap? You're not royalty. Just some chick who inherited a lot of money, through no effort of her own. I'm not one of your employees and I don't have to put up with your hoity-toity bullshit. Just fucking ask me like a normal person."

"I was!" Gaia protested.

"No one says my presence is requested unless it's coming from a lawyer. Try again."

She felt her face growing hot. She'd forgotten how this man got under her skin. "Come to the falls with me."

"I said ask, baby. Not issue orders while you're gritting your teeth. You're not better than me. You're begging for a favour."

She would not beg. Not now, not ever. "Will you fly to the falls with me?"

"Better. But you're missing the magic word."

Gaia wanted to scream. "Please."

"All together now. With feeling. Lead with the p-word."

Penis. Gaia's face grew hot.

The man was maddening, and yet his voice did things to her deep inside. Her mother would tell her not to waste her time with this rude man, to put him in his place, but Gaia didn't have to obey her mother any more. And the place she wanted him was in her bed, inside her, which meant giving in to his desires. At least, a little.

She swallowed. "Please, Jay, will you fly to the falls with me?"

"Knew you could do it! See, that didn't hurt, did it?"

The bastard was laughing at her. "Are you coming or not?"

"I never turn down a chance to do that." He chuckled, like he knew her insides heated up when she heard the double meaning in his words. "Tell me the times and I'll meet you on the helipad, baby. Figure I should see the falls. I've been here long enough."

He took down the details and ended the call.

He'd agreed. The receiver dropped from Gaia's nerveless fingers as she sighed in relief. That had been harder than she'd expected, but she'd still succeeded. He'd said it was his first trip to the falls, too, so this would all be as new to him as it was to her.

THIRTY-FOUR

"The Buccaneer Archipelago was named for an English pirate who visited them back in the seventeenth century. Name of William Dampier. Several of the bays around here are named after his ships. Cygnet Bay and Roebuck Bay. Then there's streets in town like Dampier Terrace that are called after him, too. On the east coast, they're so proud of Captain Cook, who they say was the first Englishman to explore Australia in the eighteenth century, but they're wrong. If James Cook had a hero, it was Dampier. He had copies of Dampier's journals with him on every voyage." The pilot paused to point. "If you look out that way, you'll see Cygnet Bay, where Dampier careened the Cygnet. Careening's what it's called when they haul a ship out of the water to clean all the muck off the bottom, so it can sail faster. Speed was important to a pirate ship, or they'd never catch the spice-laded Dutch ships, carrying their cargo from

Batavia back to Holland. So they'd tip the ship on its side, and scrape off all the barnacles and seaweed until the hull was clean again. With the fourteen metre tides in here, they could have floated the ship in at high tide, waited a few hours for the tide to slink out, and the ship would be left high and dry. She'd be stuck there until the tide came back in, or longer, if they judged the tides wrong and ground the ship too deeply in the soft limestone sand.

"You'd think with all our modern tide schedules, accurate charts and depth finders that wouldn't happen any more, but a couple years ago, *True South*, one of the big cruise ships grounded on a sand bar on a really high tide. It took weeks to refloat it, because the owner wanted to make sure there weren't any holes in the bottom, and with the rough conditions we get occasionally, it wasn't safe to send divers down to check. He's learned his lesson, though, and he ran week-long charters up here in the dry season for a while. The last couple of years, the boat's been floating accommodation for the construction crew at one of the oil and gas platforms off Karratha, but that's all finished now, so last I heard, he'll be offering charters again this year. If you come back in a month or two, maybe you'll be able to book one."

Gaia nodded at the pilot's commentary, tucking the information into her mind for a later date. Today she intended to enjoy herself. Work could wait.

The pilot named the islands as they passed over them, pointing out the ones that had an interesting history because of explorers or World War II. The longer they flew, the more war history he recounted, until they passed close to Lorikeet Island. He didn't touch on her island's history, but Gaia wouldn't have heard it, anyway.

Lorikeet Island drew her eye like a beacon. This was the foundation of her family fortune, and she wouldn't let it slip through her fingers. She'd promised Jay she wouldn't discuss the island today, and she wouldn't, but tomorrow she'd try again. Her fortune depended on him agreeing to her terms.

Jay mumbled something she couldn't quite hear, so she asked him to repeat it.

"Trippy trees," he said, pointing down. "When the tide's out, the rivers look like crazy trees with snakes."

Gaia looked…and laughed. Jay was right. The zigzagging riverbeds resembled snags full of snakes. Angry snakes. She'd never noticed it before.

Their flight path took them over more land than water as they headed inland. The pilot's commentary shifted from history to geology. The names of the various formations washed over her – Kimbolton, King Leopold, Fitzroy, Stokes, Talbot. All names of explorers, or wealthy people who'd financed the expeditions, sending men out to find more resources to increase their wealth. She wondered why there wasn't a Vasse something. There should be an island named after her family, at least, or a bay. Or perhaps she should petition to have the King Leopold Ranges named after her family, seeing as the man those mountains were named after had murdered millions, or so the pilot said.

Gaia snorted. He probably hadn't killed a single man, woman or child. He was a king. He gave orders to his subordinates to create a colony for him in the Congo, and they'd done it. Killing was something they'd done, out of loyalty to their leader. Yet now he was the one with a murderous reputation, and likely to lose his mountain range because of it.

"That King Leo sounds like he'd fit right in with your family. An ancestor, perhaps?" Jay grinned.

Gaia refused to rise to the bait. "He's no relation at all. My family came from England as part of a group settlement scheme. Whatever you think of me or my family, we're not murderers." She turned her back on him to stare out the window.

If only that kept his voice from reaching her ears, but the headsets made that impossible.

"You said your grandfather was in the army during World War II. Didn't he kill any Japanese troops? Or was he too important to get his hands dirty?"

Gaia's voice was flat. "I wouldn't know. He died before I was born. What does it matter, anyway? It was war, and they attacked our home. He enlisted to serve his country, like most men of the time. And when he came home, he did his best to provide for his family with what he'd learned in the army. He knew Lorikeet Island held enough iron ore to make his fortune, if he could find a way to mine it. He did, and now I'm trying to keep his dream alive, and his mine open."

She was talking about work again. What else was there, truly?

"Maybe it's time to close the mine and give the island back to its traditional owners. I heard from some of the local Aboriginal people that it was one hell of a fishing spot before your family started messing with it." Jay folded his arms behind his head. "If I wait long enough, I'll be able to buy the island off them and restart the resort with those old buildings. I might even keep that big old house for myself, so I can watch those humping whales. The whale researchers can use it when I'm not there, of course. Can't deprive the experts of the biggest live porn show on Earth."

Gaia's heart constricted in her chest. Losing Lorikeet Island to him? No. Absolutely not. She'd never let that happen. She breathed deeply, forcing herself to stay calm.

"I can't believe you haven't bitten my head off yet. My sister would have slapped me by now. Don't you ever get angry, baby?"

She turned to stare. "You mean you're baiting me on purpose? It won't work. A billionaire doesn't lose control, or they lose everything."

"So?"

Idiot. "A broke billionaire isn't a billionaire any more. They're nobody," she informed him.

To her shock, Jay just laughed. "Where do you get this shit? Some how-to book for stuck-up rich people? Or that ultra-exclusive private girls' school you went to that taught you to walk with your nose in the air? That's not how the world works. You can't control it. The sooner you learn that, the better. All you can do is take risks and hope they pay off. And if they don't, you pick yourself up, learn from your mistakes, and don't make them again. Fuck, I might be a billionaire now. I don't know. But I'll never be nobody. Never was, either. I was always me, with a plan and a dream and my music. Take away all the money and fame, and I'll still have that. Of course, if I lost all my money, nothing would take away the fact that I'm still a rock star. I could call my agent and have a new recording contract tomorrow, book a couple of tours and record another album, and I'd be back in business, raking it in again. Anyone who told you you're nobody without your money is fucked up."

Gaia wondered what her mother would have said to that. Nothing, probably. Morrigan wouldn't have listened, or she'd have pretended not to hear a word of it. What did Jay know, anyway? He hadn't been studying business and wealth principles since he could talk. He wasn't born to head a billion-dollar business. No, he'd earned his money through luck and a little talent. "You don't understand."

"I'm happy in my ignorance, baby. Hey, is that the falls coming up? It looks like the pictures we have in the hotel foyer."

The pilot confirmed that they were approaching Horizontal Falls, the only two horizontal waterfalls in the world, or so he said. Gaia didn't care to check.

"Fuck, you won't find anything like this anywhere else in the world. It's because we have the world's highest tides, I bet," Jay said.

The pilot coughed. "Second highest, at fourteen metres. There's a bay in Canada that holds the record for the highest tides. Somewhere in Nova Scotia, I'm told. And while Canada's got Niagara Falls, we have Horizontal Falls, and they're unique. At their peak, ten thousand litres of water rush through them every second. Pretty powerful, seeing as the water only falls about a metre at most. All that pressure's because the gaps it has to go through are so narrow. The smallest one's only nine metres across, while the other one's just over twenty. When the tide's right, you can take a ride in a jet boat through the falls, but it's a rough ride and it's easy to ground the boat in the shallows if you don't know what you're doing. There's a tour company that specialises in that sort of thing – they keep a floating platform in Talbot Bay where they moor the boats in the dry season, when they bring tourists out here by seaplane. They leave from the air strip at One Arm Point, if you ever want to go."

Gaia shuddered at the thought of riding that rough water – in a jet boat or a seaplane – but Jay just nodded eagerly like he couldn't wait to do it. Didn't he realise this whole place screamed DANGEROUS at the top of its lungs? Flying over it was one thing, but to be at the mercy of that strong current…

"You up for it tomorrow, baby?" Jay asked, leaning in.

"They won't fly for a few weeks yet. Not 'til the dry season, when there's enough tourists to make it worthwhile," the pilot informed them.

Gaia breathed a sigh of relief.

"I'll do a couple of low passes, so you can see the falls up close. It really is spectacular."

Before Gaia could protest, the helicopter banked, headed straight for the rocky cleft where all that fearsome water poured through. She held her breath as he hovered over it for a few minutes, repeating the numbers he'd already told them, before he flew to the second horizontal waterfall and hovered in place again.

Jay seemed fascinated by the streaming water, cascading like a waterfall that common sense told her couldn't possibly be that flat. But her eyes told her otherwise.

"Ready to head for Mitchell Falls? They're not as unique as these ones, but I promise you, they're still a sight to see. Especially at the end of a wet season like this last one. Some of the tracks are still flooded and won't be open at the start of the dry season, at this rate."

Wonderful. More nature that was too powerful to withstand. It was as if everything up here was trying to belittle her. "Sure," Gaia said.

THIRTY-FIVE

"Mitchell Falls are coming up straight ahead," the pilot said, startling Gaia out of her daydream. The monotonous landscape of red rock and scrubby trees was pierced by a new, greenish river. "Mitchell River."

Of course it was. She wondered what the pilot would say if she told him she didn't care, and she wanted to go back to the resort.

He probably wouldn't even try to talk her out of it. With a, "yes, ma'am," he'd turn around right away.

But Jay…he'd be disappointed, and he'd say so. Loudly, most likely. Then call her boring or stuck-up or something else equally insulting, with a slab of swearing slathered on top. He said what he thought, that was for sure. She'd wager he had no secrets whatsoever. In a way, he belonged here, in this wide-open landscape where everything was larger than life and unique. There was only one Horizontal

Falls, just like there was only one Jay Felix.

And Gaia Vasse? Who was she, really? Billionaire heiress, mining magnate, but she was nothing compared to the forces of nature out here. One cyclone destroyed her mine before the giant tides engulfed what remained; the rain and the rocks and the red dust conspired to wipe out the mining camp before she could begin to rebuild; and this rugged land that wanted her gone had all but embraced the man at her side, enticing him out here, weaving some sort of spell over him, before handing him everything she wanted. The resort island that would be perfect for a mining camp was his, and he wasn't selling. Lorikeet Island would slip out of her grasp forever while he tightened his hold on his glorified sand cay, a heart-shaped doughnut with no resources to distinguish it from any other island in the Buccaneer Archipelago. How come he got all the luck while hers ran out?

Life just wasn't fair.

"Did you just work that out?" Jay was laughing at her again.

Damn. She must have said that last bit out loud. She bit her lip and hoped that was the only thought she'd voiced.

"For once, you're right. Here we are, in one of the most gorgeous, untouched wildernesses in the world, with our own private helicopter and lunch laid on, while there are people who don't have enough food and water to make it through the day. Or money to pay their rent. Or time to take a day out here and really appreciate what we have. Yep, life is awesome this week, so live it up while it lasts, because next week, you could be back to looking for rent money you just don't have."

Once again, he didn't understand. Scrabbling for the money to live wasn't part of her plan.

"Incredible!" Jay breathed, pointing, and Gaia's gaze followed his finger.

The river and the whole plateau just…ended. And they were flying toward the void.

Jay cheered as they flew over the falls, no, four individual waterfalls, staggered like steps down the cliffs. Each cascade ended in its own pool, which spilled into a bigger one until the river continued on at the base of the plateau. They followed the river for a little way, before the pilot turned them around to get a better look at the spectacle that was Mitchell Falls.

Gaia had to admit it was impressive, but that only made her more miserable. Another of nature's wonders she couldn't hope to compete with. Her company mined more of this state than any other and it was barely a drop in the ocean…or a pebble on a mountain, in a mountain range that stretched forever.

"Tell me we're landing. I need to swim in that." The desire in Jay's voice was unmistakeable. Desire for a damn waterfall?

Gaia shook her head. She felt awe and insignificance, while this madman felt lust. She'd never understand him at all. Never.

THIRTY-SIX

The pilot set them down on the permanent helipad on top of the plateau. Gaia could hear the roar of the falls the moment she stuck her head out of the helicopter.

"Mitchell River and the top of the falls is a short walk that way." Shou pointed. "But the lookout and the best way to the pools is down that trail." A signpost beside a rock cairn confirmed it.

"What do you recommend first?" Jay asked.

Shou shrugged, pulling a cloth-wrapped bundle from under the seat. "See the top first, seeing as it's closer. That'll give me some time to make sure the trail's clear." He threw the cloth back into the helicopter and Gaia's eyes widened as she saw what it had covered. It looked like an old-fashioned sword belt, with a sheath and the handle of something sticking out it.

"What do you need a sword for?" she said.

Shou laughed and pulled out the blade. It looked short for a sword, and not as shiny. "It's a machete, and I'll need it to fight my way through." He slid it back into its sheath, before slinging the belt over his head, so the blade sat diagonally across his back.

Gaia backed toward the helicopter. "I didn't come here to fight people. It's too dangerous. Take me back to the resort right now."

Now both men were laughing. Shou held up his hands and attempted to explain, "No, no. Not people. Plants. It's the end of the wet season and the national park's just opened to the public this week. No one's taken this path for months, and the scrub will have tried to reclaim it. After record rains like this year, everything will have grown wild. It'll be slow going without it. And it's a steep climb back up, but I look like a bloody fool carrying that when I might need both hands to climb, so the sheath keeps it out of my way."

"I don't know why you don't get a samurai sword, like Baz suggested. The tourists would love it," Jay said.

Shou shrugged. "Perhaps. I like this blade better, though. Samurai fought people, not Australian hardwoods. A samurai blade might not be equal to one Aussie tree."

Gaia still didn't want to let go of the helicopter. The steel was a comforting piece of civilisation under her hand. Once she let go…she truly would be in the wilderness. Could she trust these men to take care of her?

"C'mon, baby. I want to stand on the top of the falls and see if I can get an echo going." Jay offered his hand.

She wanted to go home. Not just the resort, but home in Perth, where everything was familiar and not frightening.

But that would disappoint Jay, who she'd invited on this adventure. She owed it to him to at least see it through.

"I'll protect you from the plants, baby. I didn't let the mud crabs get you on the beach, though I couldn't save your shoe." Jay's grin was surprisingly reassuring. He was right, she realised. He'd carried her off the beach in the rain when she was stuck.

Reluctantly, she wrapped her fingers around his, tightening her grip as she relinquished her hold on the helicopter.

Jay hurried along the track, which ran right to the edge of the river. The cliff where it ended was frighteningly close, but Jay didn't hesitate. He waded into the water up to his knees and stood a few short metres from the edge. Cupping his hands to his mouth, he let loose a deafening, "Coo-ee!"

When no sound bounced back, he tried it again, louder still. The man sure had a decent set of lungs on him. Gaia wished she'd seen him belt out one of his songs, but Mother had always dismissed concerts as uncouth, so she'd never been to one. Now, she wished she'd flouted Mother's rules just once so she could see him perform. The gorge before him didn't faze him in the least. Gaia wondered if anything did. Not for the first time that day, she felt a pang of jealousy for the charmed life that belonged to Jay Felix.

THIRTY-SEVEN

When they returned to the landing area, they found Shou rummaging around in the back of the helicopter, no longer wearing his machete.

"That was quick," Jay remarked. "I thought you said you had to hack a path to the bottom of the falls for us. Did the trees all take one look at your mighty sword and quiver in fear?"

The pilot emerged with a picnic basket cradled in his arms. "Maybe. It wasn't anywhere near as overgrown as I'd expected. Maybe we're not the first tourists out here this season, or perhaps the park rangers decided to do their job for once and clear the track a bit for the first time in forever. I don't know. What I do know is it's a decent hike down there, but worth it. You two head on down to the lookout while I grab your lunch. I'll set it up so you'll have a good view while you eat."

"C'mon." Jay grabbed Gaia's hand again. This time she didn't hesitate when he pulled her toward the track. After all, the pilot had said it was all clear. It couldn't be that difficult a walk, surely.

Their impromptu bushwalk wasn't as hard as Gaia had expected, but she still breathed a sigh of relief when they reached the lookout. She wouldn't have put it past Jay to get lost in the surprisingly dense vegetation. It had looked so sparse from the air.

"Now this was worth it," Jay said, standing at the edge of the lookout platform and spreading his arms to encompass the view. "Almost as pretty as the view from the air."

Gaia agreed with him. From her vantage point, she could see all four waterfalls, with what looked like an offshoot stream that was far enough from the others to be considered a fifth. She felt dizzy. She'd stood at the top of that, mere metres from the lip of the uppermost cascade, but now she could see that the drop down any one of those could easily kill her.

Too big. Too dangerous. Life out here was too much for her.

"Where's your phone? Don't you want a picture of yourself standing here?" Jay demanded. "Even you have to admit this beats Lorikeet Island and you took heaps of pictures while we were out there."

Gaia fumbled for her phone and handed it to him, trying to hide the chill in heart as she realised he'd noticed her need for photographs on Lorikeet Island. What else had he noticed?

He switched places with her, taking the time to position

her perfectly before he lifted the camera to take a shot. "Smile, baby. Think of the awesome sex we're going to have later," he said.

"What?" Gaia's mouth dropped open. What had happened to being boring and bested by his own hand?

Jay waved his hands around. "Why else would you go to all this trouble, unless you wanted to try to seduce me again? It's working so far, baby. And nothing says a perfect day like sex at the end of it. Or even the middle. Not the beginning so much, because then there's really no point getting out of bed in the first place." He grinned. "Hey, tell you what. You should get a shot of us together so you'll have something else to remember me by."

Before Gaia could protest, he pulled her close with one arm as he lifted the phone with the other. "Say sex, baby," he whispered, thumbing the button on the phone.

Her blood started to simmer, rushing to her cheeks in a brilliant blush that even she could see on the phone screen. "Oh no, I look terrible!"

Jay shrugged. "Let's take a few more, then, and you work out which one's the best later."

Numbly, she nodded, then arranged her expression into a smile.

Jay clicked maybe half a dozen more shots before he grew tired and handed her phone back to her. "Looks like Shou's nearly got lunch ready. We should go get some before he eats it all."

THIRTY-EIGHT

Gaia ate mechanically, not tasting a bite of it. She couldn't have said whether she'd eaten steak or spam sandwiches. She washed it down with a cup of whatever the pilot handed to her, but she didn't taste that, either.

She stole glances at Jay, who evidently enjoyed his lunch as much as everything else they'd done today. Like everything he did in life. The man was too happy by half.

Was that why she was so attracted to him? Not just his hot body, though that was definitely enough to tempt her. It was his effortless joy at even the slightest thing, without a worry in the world. She wanted a tiny part of that.

And he'd thrown the offer of sex out so casually. She couldn't take it seriously, no matter how much she wanted to.

For all his insouciance, Jay wasn't stupid. He had noticed the photos she and the pilot had taken on Lorikeet Island.

Had he also put all the pieces together and realised why she'd wanted them?

All the more reason to keep him happy today, and make sure he enjoyed every moment. Whatever he wanted to do this afternoon, she'd be there, because she couldn't seem to stay away from him. And she didn't want to.

Jay popped an entire cake in his mouth, his cheeks bulging obscenely as he grinned. "You finished? I feel so hot, I'm dying for a swim."

Gaia rose, dusting any stray crumbs from her shirt, and nodded.

"Grab a bottle of water to take with you," Shou advised, nodding at the cooler box. "And don't swim below the bottom of the falls. Someone saw a crocodile once, so now there's signs saying it's not safe."

Crocodiles? Gaia halted. She knew they lived up here, in muddy rivers and such, but she'd never seen a wild one. Never wanted to, either.

"Is it safe to walk down there, then?" she asked. Crocodiles didn't just swim – she'd seen them sitting on riverbanks on TV.

Shou waved away her worries. "Sure. I've never seen anything bigger than a goanna here, so you should be fine. Like I said, someone thought they saw one once. If that's even true, it was probably lost, and no one's seen it since."

"Don't worry, baby," Jay added. "I'll go all Mick Dundee on you if we see one. I've wanted to wrestle a crocodile since I was a kid."

Only marginally reassured, Gaia followed Jay down the trail. And down was the predominant direction. Unlike the track from the helipad to the lookout, this one was hard going. She had to climb around or slide down rocks to keep to the path. More than once, it was on the tip of her tongue to ask Jay if they were lost, but another rock cairn would appear beside the next steep slope, marking the way, so she stayed silent. Silent except for puffing and panting, at least, and the smack of flesh every time she was forced to grab Jay's hand to steady herself or she slammed into him, breaking what would otherwise have been a bad fall. She was certainly getting a workout today, and she'd have the bruises tomorrow to prove it.

Gaia wondered if Shou would be willing to bring the helicopter down to the bottom for them, instead of making her climb all the way back up. Sliding down rocks was one thing, but climbing? Didn't you need ropes and special equipment for that sort of thing? Not to mention gloves and all sorts of protective gear. If it weren't so hot, she'd want a padded suit to protect her from the rocks right now. And gloves. She'd broken two nails already, and a third was threatening to snap. She'd have to get a manicure tomorrow for sure.

After what felt like forever, she heard Jay whooping and cheering. He must have reached the bottom. Sure enough, when she dragged her aching limbs around the bend, the trail widened out into a rock platform that ended in a murky green pool. She wanted nothing more than to immerse her body in what she hoped was cool water, but the pilot's warning echoed in her head. Crocodiles — just like the sign said. So much for a swim. She'd have a dip at the beach when they returned to the resort. And tomorrow, definitely a massage after the manicure. Even better: before the manicure.

At least she could feel the splash of the falls here. Gaia closed her eyes, letting the spray mist her skin with welcome coolness. Maybe it wasn't so bad out here after all.

"You coming for a swim, or what?"

Wait…was Jay crazy enough to swim in a river where there might be crocodiles? Gaia scanned the expanse of water before her, but he was nowhere to be seen. Had a crocodile dragged him under to his death?

Jay's laughter echoed through the gorge. "Ha! I knew I'd get decent acoustics somewhere. Would've been more fun up the top, though. You have to see this."

She finally spotted him, at the top of the final set of falls. "What are you doing up there?"

"I'm going to be swimming, unless you have a better offer." Jay disappeared from view. A moment later, he emitted a groan. Gaia wasn't sure whether the sound signified pleasure or pain.

She crossed to a ledge that looked like she might be able to step onto, and started the laborious climb. It wasn't until her shoulders were level with the top of the falls that she caught sight of Jay's head, floating on top of the pool.

He grinned at the sight of her. "I thought you'd never come. Check this place out. It's like a perfect, natural hot tub. Not too hot, not too cold, and just the right depth for incredible sex. Aren't you just dying to try it out?"

Gaia's face grew red. "Out here? Where anyone could be watching?"

Jay laughed. "Anyone? There isn't another person for miles, except for Shou, and he's busy packing up the lunch gear. After that, he'll probably watch ecchi anime under a tree on his phone, if I know him."

She was sorely tempted. The water looked cool and inviting, Jay looked hot while doing the inviting…

"Are you sure it's safe? No crocodiles?" she asked.

He shrugged. "Not certain. Let me check." He rose to his full height and Gaia realised the water was only waist deep and Jay…wasn't wearing anything below the waist. Jay sauntered across the pool, turned, and crossed it again. He did a full search pattern, wading through the water from one end to the other until he reached the bottom of the falls from the next pool up. "I'm pretty sure there's a few fish in here, but that's it," he shouted as he lifted his face to the spray.

She barely heard him, because she was too busy watching. She'd never observed a naked man in the flesh for so long before. The adult films she'd watched this week didn't count – not a single man in them looked as hot as Jay Felix did right now. With every step, the muscles in his butt flexed…and she could watch him walk all day.

"Come on up, baby. I know you want me – I can see it in your eyes."

Gaia didn't doubt it. She'd never felt so hot for a man in her life. For a few minutes, while she was in Jay's arms, the world wouldn't feel so overwhelming. She really needed that right now. All she had to do was find a way up from her current ledge to the one level with Jay's pool. Gaia surveyed the cliff, then caught a glimpse of movement below her.

She dropped her gaze to the water, where a pair of beady eyes regarded her. Eyes, snout…oh God, the monster's mouth was big enough for her to fit inside, she was sure of it.

"Crocodile!" she screamed, arms flailing as she tried to

point at it.

"Cool, really?" Jay appeared on the ledge above her, peering out. "Where? I don't see it."

Gaia glanced at the water again. The beast had disappeared. She hadn't imagined it. There was a huge crocodile lurking in the water, waiting for her to fall in so it could catch her and kill her and eat her and… She didn't want to die out here. She couldn't die out here.

She scrambled down to the rocky riverbank, her eyes never leaving the water, but the murky depths concealed the monster. Gaia sprinted across the flat and hotfooted up the trail. She scraped her shins on rocks, slid and bumped and scratched herself, but she didn't dare stop. She needed to be safe. Safe inside something man-made, where the crocodile couldn't get to her.

Her arms ached and her legs burned, but still she scrambled up the slope until the blessed helicopter came into sight. She staggered over to it and reached up to open the door. Only then did she see her hand. Every nail was broken, with only a few shreds of polish left, and it was hard to tell if those really were polish or dried blood. There was plenty of fresh blood, too, where she'd torn her nails or scraped her palms on the rocks.

"What happened to you?" The pilot rose from his seat under a shady tree, staring. "Did you fall over one of the falls? Or did Jay do that?" His expression darkened.

Gaia couldn't seem to catch her breath to speak, so she shook her head, fighting to form words. "C-c-crocodile. I saw it. Huge. In the water." She couldn't stop shaking.

"Okayyyy. I'm going to get the first aid kit, so we can get you cleaned up a bit." Shou cracked open the helicopter door and spread a towel on the floor. "You just sit here on this towel, and I'll take care of you."

She did as she was bid, too exhausted to do much else. Even the disinfectant didn't sting that much, she was so out of it.

"Drink this," the pilot ordered, pushing a cup into her band-aided hand.

Obediently, Gaia emptied the cup, feeling the burn of bubbles as the liquid cascaded down her throat. The cup fell from her fingers, but somehow it came back, full again, so she drank some more. Didn't matter what, as long as she was in the safety of the helicopter. Where crocodiles couldn't reach her.

"Put this on."

Darkness engulfed Gaia until the pilot pulled the t-shirt over her head fully. She slipped numb fingers through the sleeves and pulled the hem down. It was a cheap souvenir shirt from Broome, big enough to fit two of her, and bearing an eye-wateringly bright image of a bloke on a beach with a beer in hand. She wouldn't be seen dead in it at home, but now it took away the chill she couldn't seem to shake.

When it looked like the pilot was finished with her – or he'd run out of band-aids, she wasn't sure – Gaia crawled onto the seat furthest from the door and curled up. She wasn't getting out of the helicopter until they reached civilisation, or at least the resort.

THIRTY-NINE

Jay's jubilant voice pierced Gaia's black mood. "Pencil it in, mate – I want a regular charter out here, once a week, for as long as I'm living at the resort. Can't believe I haven't been out here before."

The pilot replied, his voice too low for Gaia to discern the words.

She stretched, cautiously putting her feet down so she could slide closer to the door to hear their conversation.

"A crocodile? Fuck, yeah, there was! I didn't see it when she started screaming, so I stayed to swim for a while, but when I was done, I saw it. It was basking on the river bank, fast asleep. I thought it was a log at first, until I realised it had a tail." Jay laughed. "Dunno what she was so afraid of, though. It was only little. Maybe two metres from nose to tail. It probably would've weighed less than her, too. I could've taken it, easy."

Gaia didn't want to hear any more, but the pilot's voice intruded anyway.

"You better not try it. The police will arrest you for croc wrestling, because it gives the tourists ideas. There used to be a wildlife park in town with some real big crocodiles, but some idiot got drunk at Diver's Tavern one night and decided to get friendly with the biggest one in the park. Climbed the fence, jumped into the croc's pond and he was lucky to make it out alive when the caretaker heard the ruckus. They moved the park to Ten Mile after that. Now there's just the remains of the enclosures behind Zookeeper's in Cable Beach, and the same grumpy caretaker to keep trespassing tourists out."

Jay laughed so hard he doubled over, slapping his thigh.

The sound sent a jolt through to Gaia's core, waking her up.

"Sounds like something I'd do sober, and then get drunk afterwards. Speaking of which, you got any more beer in the esky? I wouldn't mind one as part of the inflight catering on the way back."

Gaia retreated to her corner as Jay cracked open the door. He glanced at her, before ignoring her completely as he rooted around in the cooler box behind the seat. He ducked out with his can of beer, then climbed into the co-pilot's seat. As far away from her as possible, like she had some sort of disease to be avoided at all costs. Cowardice wasn't contagious. Just...embarrassing.

When the pilot joined them, Jay jerked his head in Gaia's direction without looking at her. "Thanks for handling all the first aid and stuff. It's not really my thing."

Gaia's rock-bottom mood sank to subterranean depths.

So much for sex later – Jay didn't want to touch her now.

"No worries," the pilot replied, slipping on his headset.

Jay did the same, but Gaia didn't bother with hers. She didn't want to hear anything they had to say, and she hoped the roar of the rotors would drown out her own thoughts. For the first time in her life, she wanted to drown her sorrows in a bottle. As soon as she reached civilisation.

A familiar beep roused her from her doze. That sound signified an email, her foggy mind told her, and that meant they were within range of a phone tower. As if to prove her point, the helicopter tilted sideways and Gaia caught a glimpse of buildings nestled between palm trees before all she could see was the aqua blue of the lagoon. The resort. Thank goodness.

She tapped her phone screen, hoping the email would provide a welcome distraction until her feet touched solid ground again.

Her hopes were dashed when she saw it was an urgent message from Stewart about Lorikeet Island.

Gaia was tempted to ignore it, but twenty-five years of her mother's mantra – business always comes first – squelched that idea before it had fully formed.

Sighing, she opened the email. The text was brief: he needed her written approval for mass layoffs at the mine. Every day she delayed, they'd be paying for workers they no longer needed for a closed mine.

No. Closing the mine meant losing the island.

Tears blurred her vision until she couldn't see the message from Stewart any more.

No. She couldn't cry. She hadn't shed a tear at her mother's funeral. She couldn't...

…couldn't take it any more. She was too spent after the day to do anything to stop the tears from cascading down her cheeks, a poor imitation of the falls today. And just like the falls, they kept on flowing.

"What's wrong, baby?" Jay sounded worried.

"I don't want to lose my island," she whispered. "Grandfather and Mother will never forgive me."

Jay snorted. "Baby, last time I checked, they were both too dead to care what you do with your island."

His insensitive statement was enough to push her into action. "Leave me alone," Gaia ordered, shoving the door open so she could make her escape. Her stiff muscles protested after sitting so long, but she was determined to make it to her villa before anyone else could see her cry.

Jay and the pilot were bad enough. After all, she wouldn't be in this mess if it weren't for Jay. If he'd just sign the contract and hand over the resort, instead of being such a stubborn jackass…

Gaia gave an almighty sniff, lifting her head high, before marching back to the privacy of Villa Maxima.

FORTY

Xan had to dial Jay's number twice, she was so excited. This was by far the biggest deal she'd ever brokered, and it was an impressive coup even for Romance Island Resort. Her dream of organised day trips to the island would become a reality in a matter of weeks. She'd already floated the idea past the high-end resorts in Broome at Cable Beach and Roebuck Bay, and they'd been interested in offering the tours to their guests. She'd met the cruise ship operators at the travel fair, and they'd jumped at the idea, but the ships docked for less than a dozen days a year, so even if they booked out their tours on those days, it would hardly make a dent.

But having resident mine crew next door, looking to do something on their days off, but with the money to be able to afford a boat charter…Xan suppressed a squeal of delight. The resort would have a record profit this high season. All because of her.

When Jay answered his phone, she sang out, "It's done! Signed, sealed and delivered! We have a deal with Vasse Prospecting that'll cut the day trip costs in half while bringing us hundreds of new customers during rebuilding and when the mine's operational again!" Xan wanted to dance.

"So that's good news, then?" Jay asked.

"Sure is! Oh, and I ordered some new sunbeds. The new ones at the Mangrove Hotel were a big hit with guests, so I got the name of their supplier and they should already be on the way up by road train, arriving tomorrow. Can you check to make sure they're installed as soon as they arrive? There's one for each villa, plus a few more for the new decking outside the Jungle."

"Mm-hmm." Jay didn't sound all that excited. Well, he hadn't seen them yet. Once he had, she probably wouldn't be able to get him off them.

"Sorry, am I keeping you from your latest conquest?" she snapped.

"Nah, just distracted, is all. If the news is so good, why was Gaia so upset today? She received a message on her phone and looked like someone had died. Is there anyone in her family left?"

"No, she's the last surviving Vasse, thank goodness. Maybe she broke a nail." Xan shook her head. "Who knows? Or maybe she saw the news about her in the gossip magazines. I don't read those things, so I don't know what they said, just that she's on the cover of all of them this week. Not my problem, anyway. I'm off to grab a celebratory drink. To Romance Island Resort's rosy future!"

Jay laughed. "Yeah, I might go up to the pub and do the same. Good work. Thanks, Xan."

159

FORTY-ONE

The bottle of white wine in her fridge was empty far too quickly, and it didn't dull her feelings fast enough. Not enough alcohol, she was certain of it. If Gaia had been a bourbon drinker, or if she'd liked any spirits, she'd have ordered a bottle to be delivered direct to her villa. Room service must have something appropriate for getting drunk, she grumbled to herself as she picked up the phone.

"I'm sorry, ma'am, but we don't have any cocktails on the room service menu," the waiter on the other end said once she'd explained what she wanted. "What with the heat and the distance from the bar to your villa, they don't travel well. If you give me a list of your preferred cocktails, I can send a bartender over with the ingredients and he can make those for you in the privacy of your villa."

"Do that then," Gaia snapped.

"The earliest I can get an extra bartender to the island is

next week, ma'am. It being the wet season and all, we only have the one barman and he's stuck in the Jungle all week."

"Then send someone to pick him up." Why did things have to be so hard?

The waiter laughed, which turned quickly into a cough. "Lots of people try, ma'am, but I understand Marcel's happily married. If you want cocktails tonight, your best bet is to head up to the hotel and see the Jungle for yourself. That's the hotel bar, ma'am."

Getting drunk in a public bar. Morrigan would turn over in her grave at the thought of her daughter doing something so disgraceful. But Mother would disapprove even more when Gaia lost Lorikeet Island. What was one night in a bar?

Gaia glanced down at her clothes. She'd changed out of the hideous t-shirt, and the ripped, stained clothes she'd worn underneath were in the rubbish, where they belonged. She looked presentable enough in her current outfit – more items from that resort collection she'd never had an excuse to wear until now. Her tears had long since dried and ice had taken care of the tell-tale puffiness that would proclaim to the world that Gaia Vasse had been crying. No one deserved to know her feelings. When she entered the bar tonight, her frigid façade would be unbreachable.

She strapped on her sandals and sallied forth into the night, relishing the way the humidity caressed her skin. Had it always done that, or was it just something in the air tonight?

Gaia was surprised to find the hotel bar almost empty. A couple sat at a corner table, completely engrossed in one another, and the only other person she could see was the cheery bartender. She wove between the potted palms until she found a table that was surrounded by enough jungle to hide her from the other bar patrons. Sinking into the cane chair, she almost jumped right back out again when she discovered the bartender right next to her.

He didn't look the slightest bit fazed. "What can I get you?"

"The cocktail menu."

He reached across the table and laid a laminated card in front of her. "There you are. Which one would you like?"

No one in the whole damn Kimberley understood her. "All of them. The whole menu."

He laughed like he thought she was joking.

She wasn't.

His laughter died, but a professional smile remained. "Any particular order, or a favourite you want to start with?"

Gaia stared unseeingly at the menu before her. "Just go down the list, and keep them coming."

"And you, sir?"

"A cold beer. And don't you dare put an umbrella or a straw in it." Jay slid into the seat across from Gaia. "You are not drinking your way through the whole cocktail menu."

"I'm a grown woman. I can drink whatever I want," she retorted.

Jay laughed. "Sure, right up until you get so drunk Marcel won't serve you any more. Medical evacuation for alcohol poisoning isn't pretty, and it's hardly responsible service of alcohol, which Marcel prides himself on."

If she ignored him, would he leave?

She kept her silence until the drinks arrived – the first

cocktail on the menu was something called a fluffy duck, she found, which smelled of rum and coconut and all things tropical. Everything she usually loved about her rare holidays, but not this time.

"Better get us some food to go with this. Whatever you got, mate. This one's a lightweight. A couple of glasses of champagne the other night and she was on her ear," Jay told the barman, who nodded and hurried off to obey Jay's orders.

"I can handle my liquor just fine, thank you. And I'll eat when I'm damn well ready, not because you say so." Gaia took a deep pull from her straw. The potent cocktail made her eyes water, but she blinked the tears away. She refused to show any more weakness in front of Jay.

"Who said the food's for you? If I'm going to have to carry your drunk arse back to your house, I'll need to keep my strength up."

His grin clawed at her misery. "Go away."

He didn't seem to have heard her. "You know, the tables over the other side have a better view of the stars. They're pretty spectacular out here."

Like the waterfalls and the mountains and everything else that made her feel far too insignificant for her liking? "No thanks. I don't like stars."

Jay laughed. "How can anyone not like stars? Brilliant balls of gas, burning far away with nuclear power we can barely imagine, but just pinpricks in our sky here. I love to stand out on the beach and just watch the whole Milky Way. Someone told me the local Aboriginal people here call it the Big Emu. When I've had enough to drink, I can almost see it. You gotta kind of blur your eyes, lie back and look up. Makes you really feel one with the universe and all that shit. Being a star myself and all."

Jay meandered on, telling her stories about his life as a rock star. The roadies, the concerts, the other bands, the things that went on behind the scenes that most people never heard about, along with the times the press did hear about stuff that they blew out of all proportion.

"So many times they called me a rock god in the news, and most of the time it's all bullshit, but there's only one…nah, maybe two bits of the job where they're right. The first is when you're recording an album. At first, it's all kinda dark, void, formless, barely an idea of what will become. And there's the sound engineer telling you to make music, so out of nothing, you say to yourself, 'Let there be music,' and there it is. By the time you're finished, you've created something entirely new, and it's good."

Gaia finished her second…or was it her third? She couldn't remember. Anyway, she drank the last of her whatever-number fluffy duck, then snorted as she realised why Jay's words were so familiar, even if he'd bastardised the quote.

"What?" Jay demanded.

"Sounds like something out of the Book of Genesis. I didn't think someone like you would know anything about the Bible."

Jay stiffened. "What, you think only rich snobs like you get to go to private religious schools? I got news for you, baby. I went to a private Catholic school, and so did my sister. The whole band did."

Gaia's eyes widened in surprise. She almost missed the table with her empty glass, but corrected in time. "I just thought…you went to a public school or something. The way you call me a snob, like it's some sort of insult to take pride in yourself, and your family, and – "

Jay snorted. "I take pride in myself and my fucking family, but I'm not up myself like you, baby. I know who I am, which is more than I can say for you. Your family and your teachers have puffed you up so much with your own self-importance, they forgot to tell you that you have to be yourself first. You're not your family or your money or your fucking island. Who you are is about what you do. What you create, what you protect, what you make of your life. What other people will remember you for. If you don't do anything, you're nothing."

Tears sprang to her eyes. Gaia blinked and blinked, but somehow she lost the battle. She ducked her head to hide her wet cheeks from Jay.

She was nothing. She couldn't even protect her family's island. Nothing.

"Go away!" she ordered.

"What's wrong, baby?"

Those words again. Spoken in a low voice, filled with concern. No one cared about her. No one.

Gaia raised her head, expecting to see Jay's maddening grin, but the man wore a frown. She met his eyes, wondering at his questioning look. Yes, questioning – not calculating, like most men were when they sensed weakness.

Jay didn't want anything from her. That was the difference. Every other man she'd been with wanted to possess her or get her to give them something. He sat across from her because he wanted to be here, and all he wanted was the answer to his question.

She'd made enough of a fool of herself in front of him today.

Gaia shoved her chair away from the table and rose. All the ducks swimming in the rum in her bloodstream flew into her head, blinding her with their fluffiness.

Strong arms caught her before her wobbly knees threw her onto the floor. "Time to get you home, baby."

Civilisation. Where the world didn't make her feel so small. "I want to go home." But her legs weren't working properly. Too much running. Crocodiles and now ducks. "Where wildlife won't attack me."

Jay's chuckled rumbled through his chest. Through her, as she was pressed against it. "I'm a match for all the wildlife here. They know I'm the king of this island."

King of the island. Did that make her the queen of Lorikeet? "We should marry. Queen of Lorikeet and King of Romance. Bring the kingdom together. I'll mine the rocks and you romance the whales." Perfect. Perfect plan.

"You're drunk." Jay scooped her up in his arms and headed out into the dark. "Stop wiggling or I'll get Maintenance to bring a wheelbarrow. I can't just leave you here, and I won't carry you if you're struggling like a fresh-caught fish."

Gaia squirmed a bit more until she was comfortable. "No one else has ever carried me like this.Feels…weird." A thought brought a smile to her lips. "Are you carrying me off to bed to ravish me?"

"Oh, so now you want sex? Make up your mind, will you? Most girls run screaming toward me, not away. You confuse people and there'll be trouble."

"I confuse you?" Hope welled up in her chest. If she

intrigued Jay, maybe he would want something from her. Something personal.

"You? No, baby. You're about as transparent as they come. To me, anyway. Nah, but you might have given the pilot the wrong idea today when you ran away from me. I don't hurt women. Never. He got the wrong idea once when I was role playing a bit with a girl. He tried to get me arrested for having a bit of fun. Consensual fucking fun. Fuck, she wanted it more than I did! I tried telling him that, but…heh. Got him back, though. Christened his helicopter and left him a present on the seat. He won't try that again."

Gaia's fuzzy mind wondered what he'd been doing. Maybe one of the things she'd seen the actors doing in those porn films she'd watched. Did anyone really do that stuff in real life? If anyone did, it'd be Jay.

More than ever, she wished she could remember the night they spent together. Five times…if only she had more than vague memories of even one, or she could separate the bits that were real from the bits that she dreamed afterwards.

Maybe he'd be willing to do it again tonight. He was carrying her to bed, wasn't he?

He swiped his wristband on the security panel and the door hissed open. Jay carried her over the threshold of what she was surprised to find was her villa, not his. How'd he manage to unlock her door?

Jay set her down on the couch, then headed to the kitchen. Gaia heard water running, but her eyes weren't on him. They were on the stack of papers on her dining table — the contract Jay still hadn't signed.

If he didn't sign them tonight, she'd have to let Stewart

close down the mine in the morning. Her first big challenge as chairman and she'd failed. Failed her family, failed herself, failed to negotiate the simplest of deals. A lifetime of learning to run Vasse Prospecting and barely a fortnight into the job, she'd demonstrated that she was a failure.

And Mother wasn't here to fix it.

"Here, drink this." Jay held out a pint glass full of water.

Too tired to argue, Gaia wrapped both hands around the glass and drank. But as fast as she replenished it, more water leaked out of her eyes. Tears of grief, tears of shame, tears of sorrow for all she'd lost and things she'd never have.

When it all became too much, she laid her head down on the couch and sobbed. No amount of alcohol would take this pain away. No amount of anything would help.

She cried until she had no tears left, and her mouth was so dry she needed another drink. Gaia lifted her head off the couch, peering at the glass to see if there was any water left.

The glass was full. Not half full or a quarter full – brimming to the top full, with a jug of iced water bleeding condensation on the table beside it. She sat up and stared.

Jay shifted from his seat on the couch across from her. "Feel better?"

Gaia shook her head. To stop herself from wailing in misery that he'd witnessed her weakness yet again, she gulped down the contents of the glass. And another.

"Is there anything you'd like me to do, to help you feel better?"

Raise Morrigan from the dead and put her back in charge of the company. Go back in time and stop the sea wall from breaking. Teach her how to get out of this mess. Make today never have happened, so she wouldn't feel like such a failure.

Gaia eyed the accusing pile of papers, topped with a page bearing a blank line where his signature should be. "You could sign that."

His eyes widened. "I was thinking more along the lines of a quickie on the couch, but I could do that, if you prefer. If it'd help."

Was he joking? After all their arguing and his stubborn resistance, now he was willing to sign them?

"So if I asked you whether you wanted sex or my autograph on your papers over there, you only want my autograph?" Jay didn't look like he believed her.

Not even a night of the most incredible, mind-blowing sex would make up for the magnitude of her failure if he didn't sign the agreement. Because in the morning, she'd still be a failure.

"Yes," she whispered. She farewelled his gorgeous body with her eyes.

"All right, then." Jay picked up a pen, clicked it once, and scrawled his signature. "So you're okay now? Don't need anything else from me?"

Gaia shook her head, unable to believe her eyes.

"G'night then." Whistling, Jay ambled out of the villa.

FORTY-TWO

When Gaia woke up on the couch the next morning, her eyes darted first to the table, to see if the papers were still there. Yes, they were.

Groggily, she clambered to her feet, wincing as every bit of her body protested. Actually, not every bit. Her head seemed remarkably pain free, even after the amount she'd drunk last night. It must have been all the water she'd gulped down after she got home. Huh. Water as a hangover cure. Who'd have guessed?

She staggered stiffly over to the table to check that Jay really had signed the contract. Yep, his autograph spilled over half the page, all curlicues and flourishes and finished with a kiss – or at least an x. Gaia snorted. So much for a businesslike signature like she'd cultivated for two decades. Jay made a performance out of it, like he did everything else.

Show off. Whooping in the jet boat in Yampi Sound, shouting across the gorge at Mitchell Falls, and even suggesting sex in that pool between the cascades, like he wanted the whole world to see how good he was.

He loved it up here. The islands, the landscape, the wildlife…it was all larger than life, just like him. And it left her aching, just like he did.

Gaia made herself a cup of tea and sat at the table, pulling the papers toward her. What had made him sign them? After all his arguing, he'd agreed without a murmur last night. She wished she'd been thinking more clearly, but those cocktails had fuzzied her brain something awful. She should have invited him back to her bedroom to celebrate the agreement. Then she'd still be in his arms, instead of clenching her thighs against the aching emptiness inside.

How much beer had Jay had to drink last night? Was he drunk, too?

She scrutinised the signature. It looked clear and unwavering, more readable than her own on a good day. But then, Jay had spent the last six years autographing anything his fans thrust at him. He could probably manage a legible signature no matter how much he'd had to drink. It must be a rock star thing.

So he could sign stuff drunk. But did that mean he understood what he'd agreed to? What if he hadn't?

Gaia's blood ran cold. If she tricked him out of the island he loved, he'd never speak to her again. Never look at her the way he had last night. Sex would certainly be off the table. And she'd lose the only man who cared for her, not her money. Because he didn't need it.

Oh God. What had she done?

FORTY-THREE

The whole time she was in the shower, Gaia debated with herself over what she should do. Stewart expected to receive her response to his request to fire the mine staff today. She could surprise him with Jay's signed agreement instead, showing him once and for all that she did have all of her mother's business acumen and more, but Jay would hate her for it.

She needed to ask him. Somehow, she needed to get him to tell her whether he'd meant to sign away his island last night, or whether it had been a mistake. If his agreement was just the alcohol talking, she owed it to him to get out of the deal. After all, he hadn't taken advantage of her drunken state last night. He'd taken care of her to the point of carrying her home. Not to mention his surprise hangover cure. She owed him the same courtesy.

Gaia dressed in subdued colours today, covering more

skin than she normally would in such a hot climate, but her numerous cuts and scrapes were a painful reminder of how much of a fool she'd been yesterday. And she didn't want to remember. Today was a new day, and she had obligations to fulfil.

Sunglasses were a must in today's glaring sunlight, but Gaia decided against a hat for the short walk to Villa Penguin.

When she arrived, she found a cleaning cart outside the wide open door. Maid service meant Jay was out, she decided, and she'd made it halfway down the veranda steps before she heard his unmistakeable laughter from inside the villa.

Was he doing the maid? Half horrified, half intrigued, Gaia ventured through the open door. If she caught them in the act, she'd owe him nothing, she told herself. A man who turned her down only to sleep with the domestic staff wasn't worth her time, or her concern. She should take his island off him to stop him from sexually harassing his staff.

"Good morning!" Jay called before Gaia spotted him. He sat on the couch, coffee in hand, looking like he'd never heard of a hangover, let alone had one. "I was just waiting for Jackie to finish before I brought you a present." He waved in the direction of his dining alcove, where a middle-aged maid frowned deeply as she wrapped a package in paper printed with the resort logo.

She recovered quickly from her disappointment at not catching him in the act. Nobody bought her presents any more. At least, not personal ones. Boring corporate gifts from clients and contractors didn't count. Her fingers itched to tear away the packaging before the maid had finished taping it together.

"There. Done." The maid's eyes darted from Gaia to Jay. "Do you still want me to deliver it to her place, or are you going to give it to her yourself now? Because if you've got a visitor, I might pop over to Villa Maxima and clean there first."

Jay shrugged. "Suit yourself. Come back and kick us out of here when you need to."

A maid would never have been allowed to interrupt a conversation in her mother's house, let alone ask them to leave so she could clean. They were servants, at least while they were on duty. Their job was to be invisible, not join in the conversation. Jay didn't seem to have a problem with it, though.

"Thanks for doing the wrapping," Jay continued, crossing the room to retrieve the package. "Never could wrap shit to save my life. Those Christmas gift-wrapping services in shopping centres were the only reason anyone ever got wrapped presents from me. Or I bribed my sister to do it for me."

"Wouldn't surprise me," the maid muttered on her way out.

Gaia wasn't sure what to make of that exchange. Finally, she said, "You're very familiar with your staff."

"Of course. When I see them every day, I should be. Jackie's son's training to be a pilot. When he's qualified, he wants a job flying tourists around the Kimberley. He's already promised to take me up for some aerobatics when he's next in Broome." Jay grinned in anticipation. "Lee from Maintenance swore he'd let me know when we get another tiger shark in the lagoon so I can help fish it out. Usually, he likes to fight the big fish himself, but the last one took a bite out of the boat, so we needed a new one. Seeing as I had to pay for the new gear, I want to be there when we get to test it out."

"So retirement at the resort isn't like being a rock star, then?" she asked. "I can't imagine you associating with the road crew the way you do with the people here."

Jay burst out laughing. "We got to work on your imagination, then. Fuck, I knew all the roadies by name, and their girlfriends and wives, too. Had to, so I wouldn't sleep with them when the guys were busy. Some of those girls weren't the faithful type, but I didn't want any bad blood between me and the blokes. The other reason was security. Our security specialist drummed it into us from the beginning – if we didn't know someone on the crew, report them before they could become a risk. Not to me, so much, but the girls in the band."

Gaia knew Jay was the lead singer of Chaya, but she hadn't known much about the other band members. "There were girls in your band?"

"Haven't you ever seen us play?" When Gaia shook her head, he continued, "Guess that explains it, then. Chaya was me and the girls. Jojo and Angel. Big on security, both of them. And privacy. So I did most of the press and promotional stuff, and I got along well with all the guys. It's a bit like family when you're on tour."

Staff were never family. Not in her house. Gaia found herself shaking her head at the strange world Jay lived in. Or had lived in.

"You're distracting me, baby. I meant to give you these last night, but I forgot. Better late than never, though." He held out his present.

The package was surprisingly heavy. Books, Gaia decided, as she carefully removed the wrapping. If she'd expected antique first editions, she was sadly disappointed. Instead, there were three paperbacks that didn't even look new. She examined the cover of the first one, which bore a picture of a grey tie. *Fifty Shades of...* "WHAT?" she yelped. "Is this some sort of sick joke?"

"Dunno if that's what the author had in mind when she wrote it, seeing as I heard it was originally fanfiction of some kids' book, but I figured it'd be educational for you."

Gaia stabbed a finger at the stack of books. He'd given her the whole trilogy. "These are romance books. The sort of books ordinary women read to liven up their boring lives. People like me don't have time for this…this…pulp. My reading time is for business books. Educational books, as you put it, that can actually teach me things that might be useful in life."

Jay's expression grew thoughtful. "Oh, I think you can learn plenty from romance books. Especially about livening things up, baby." His eyes flashed. "Maybe this is why what you call ordinary women are so awesome in bed, and girls like you wouldn't know which bit goes where. People like you should make time for romance books, because life without a bit of romance is what's boring. You don't know the first thing about billionaires, except that you happen to be one. Broaden your horizons, baby. Find out what rich people are really like."

"Romance books are nothing like real life," Gaia replied weakly.

"Have you ever read one?" Jay demanded, not waiting

for an answer before he went on, "Jackie's read every one in the resort library, she tells me, so I asked her to start you off easy. She's been working here at the villas since the resort opened. She's met more VIPs than I have, and that's saying something. And she says the kinky stuff they get up to…well, the books barely scratch the surface. Particular tastes? She's seen things that make me look like a monk in comparison." He wrapped the paper loosely around the books again and thrust the package at her chest. "Here, take it home and get reading. If you want more, head to the resort library. And when you're done, if you want to really lose control and try a ride on the kinky side, then come back here and find me."

Jay turned her round and marched her down the passage to his front door. He waved it open, and pushed her out onto the veranda. "I'm partial to a pair of handcuffs, personally," he said before the door slid shut.

Gaia wanted to throw the books on the ground and hammer on his door until he opened it again. She held her wristband up to his scanner, but it only gave her error messages and didn't open. Damn Jay Felix. If he wouldn't let her back in, she wouldn't ask him about the contract he'd signed.

It wasn't until she stormed back inside her own house that she realised she still clutched the books to her chest. She dropped them on her own dining table, determined to tell the maid to take them back where she got them.

Before she could open her mouth, she heard the woman say, "Bloody good books there. They were my first introduction to BDSM erotica. When you're done with them, let me know, and I'll get you something a bit hotter.

Or if you're feeling a bit experimental…check the room service menu in the bedside cabinet. This is Romance Island Resort, after all. We cater to all tastes."

Gaia spluttered. What sort of woman did the maid think she was? Before she could ask, the woman was gone.

FORTY-FOUR

Gaia's walk on the beach did little to calm the storm inside. There was plenty of anger at Jay and his staff, but underneath it she still worried about the contract. She couldn't send it without asking him, but she couldn't look at him without wanting to slap him.

Like he'd slapped her that night they spent together…

Her core muscles clenched at the thought of how hot that had been. That slight sting, tingling on her bottom, sending sparks deep inside her.

No, she didn't want to slap his backside. She wanted to slap his face.

And feel his hand on her bottom…was it simply his touch that had aroused her so much, or was it the slap itself? It's not like anyone had ever slapped her before. Not even children at school when she was little – Gaia had never attended a school where violence occurred.

What if…

The sound of her phone ringing inside the house startled her out of her unsettling thoughts. By the time the door slid open and she'd made it to the phone, she'd missed a call from Stewart.

Gaia considered ignoring it, but she knew she couldn't. He'd only call back.

She hit the return call button on her screen and waited a moment for the call to connect.

"How's your holiday?" Stuart greeted her.

It was on the tip of her tongue to tell him she wasn't on holiday, but Gaia swallowed and said instead, "Hot. With beaches and cocktails."

"It's rained all week here. Autumn is awful. I wouldn't mind a tropical holiday, but some of us have to work for a living." Stewart sounded bitter. "I called because I sent you an email and you haven't replied. Your mother insisted on approving all shutdowns and layoffs when this many staff are involved, but it's really only a formality. All the notices are drafted and ready to go tomorrow, but I need your approval in writing today or we'll have to recalculate all the severance pay and it'll cost much more. The company can't afford a delay, not with production halted at Lorikeet Island and current prices. The Chinese market – "

"I got your email." Gaia kept her tone emotionless. "Is it really necessary to close the mine?"

Stewart laughed as if she'd made a joke. "Miss Vasse, the mine at Lorikeet Island is under water. Twenty metres of it, I'm told. Unless you're aware of an underwater mining technique that you'd like to try?" More condescending laughter. "That won't change our need to let the current staff go. None of them are trained in your magical new technology."

Gaia gritted her teeth. "I'll give you a response by the end of the day. Is there anything else I should know?"

"Nothing worth bothering you about while you're on holiday. Just leave the business of running the company to me."

She'd had enough of his smooth voice, so she ended the call. Gaia wanted to smash the phone on the floor, but she knew it wouldn't help. It was Stewart's face she wanted to smash, and she'd never do anything so crass. No, the only way to get rid of him was to force him into early retirement. Why couldn't Stewart have been the one to succumb to a heart attack in his sleep, instead of Morrigan?

Then she wouldn't have to worry about what to do with the contract sitting on her dining table. For Mother, the answer would have been simple: the company came first. Always.

But Mother had never wanted a man as much as Gaia wanted Jay Felix right now. She would never have understood.

What she wouldn't give to have someone to talk to about these things, but billionaires didn't have friends like ordinary people. They had staff…and they had family.

So Gaia called the only member of her family left.

FORTY-FIVE

"Hello, Daddy."

"Hi, sweetheart. How are you holding up?"

Gaia took a deep breath, then counted to five as she released it slowly. "I wish Mother was still alive."

"Me, too. She was taken too young." He cleared his throat. "I thought it'd be me to go first, not her."

Gaia felt like someone had punched her in the stomach. "Oh no, Daddy. I couldn't bear to lose you. Then I wouldn't have anyone to talk to." She swallowed. "I wish you'd come to the funeral."

"You know she wouldn't have wanted me there."

She knew, but that didn't mean she understood. "Why? I know you two didn't get along and you parted ways so many years ago I barely remember the two of you in the same house together, but it's not like she would have actually seen you. I wanted you there." Her voice was plaintive. Yes, even weak, but her father was the only person who would never take advantage of her weakness. He loved her.

A sigh. "I know, sweetheart, but I'd like to think that there's something after death and Morrie…it's what she would have wanted. She wanted no further contact with me and I respected that, even though I didn't like it."

Morrie. Only Chris Grey had ever called her mother that. Morrigan had never referred to him by name, as far back as Gaia could remember. He'd always been "your father" on the rare occasions when the words had issued from Morrigan's pursed lips.

"Why, Daddy?" She'd asked him so many times why her mother hadn't allowed her to spend much time with her father, but he'd never answered. Not properly, anyway. Until she'd turned eighteen, he'd been allowed to send her birthday and Christmas presents, and occasionally there'd been a telephone call. Now, the calls were more frequent, but it didn't make up for the years she hadn't seen him.

"Because your mother didn't want me to corrupt you with what she called my sentimentality. You needed to be one of the best business minds in the world to be able to manage her company in the years ahead, and that meant hard thinking. She said I'd make you soft." He laughed. "Talk about switching gender roles. Boys used to be taken from their mothers to be trained as warriors, future fighting men, who showed no weakness. But Morrie always got her way, and it was the same with you. She wanted her hard little chairman-in-training, and I knew it was the best way to help you with your financial future, so I stayed away. She could make you one of the richest women in the world, just like her. Morrie and I both wanted the best for you. Is financial security such a bad thing? It's harder to be happy without it."

"It's hard to be happy at all," Gaia said.

"What's wrong, sweetheart?"

"With Mother gone, everything falls to me. The company, dealing with that odious managing director, and there was an accident at one of the mines…"

Chris made sympathetic noises. "So the seawall at Lorikeet Island finally gave way? It was only a matter of time. I told your mother she needed to do something about it. So did James Stewart, but she didn't like listening. Sometimes you have to think longer term than the next ore shipment."

Gaia found herself nodding. "What should I do, Daddy?"

"You're asking me? I've never managed a mine, sweetheart. I'm better sticking to real estate and property management. But if you were one of my clients, who'd just lost a building in some sort of disaster, I'd ask you: can you rebuild?"

"Well, yes, but – "

"Does it make financial sense to rebuild?" Chris interrupted. "When there was that big earthquake in Christchurch a few years back, one of my clients did lose a substantial high-rise. Insurance would have covered the cost of rebuilding, but building approval would take a long time, and he wouldn't receive any of the rental income from the tenants whose building had come down until the new one was finished. He invested his money elsewhere instead, and sold the Christchurch property, or what was left of it. The new investment in Perth…it doubled in value in that time, all the while bringing in a steady rental income. Sometimes you have to cut your losses to see a profit. Have you even seen Lorikeet Island?"

"Yes. I'm out in the Buccaneer Archipelago now, on one of the nearby islands where there's a resort. We flew out there a few days ago and it's a mess. There's nothing left of the sea wall. The airstrip's gone and buried most of the mining camp and the port's cut off from the island by the deep water over what used to be the mine." She drew a deep breath. "But Mother said of all the assets she owned, she'd never lose Lorikeet Island. It was our luck."

Chris chuckled. "Morrie always was superstitious. She hated black cats and ladders, and spilling salt. I remember her crossing the street to get away from a cat once. It wasn't even black. Sort of a mottled, black and brown moggy. But she wouldn't take the risk, so across the road she went."

"But it was where Grandfather first made the family fortune. That made it special." Even in Gaia's ears, the reasoning sounded weak. Funny. It never had when Morrigan had said it.

"Sounds like Morrie being sentimental, when she swore she was hard as nails. Your first investment is just a stepping stone to the next, nothing more."

"Did you keep your first?" Gaia pressed.

Chris cleared his throat. Stalling, perhaps. "I kept it for twenty years, and then an opportunity arose to sell that was too good to pass up. A development nearby needed the land and my little townhouses were in the way. They offered me market value at first, but I knew the development couldn't go ahead if they didn't have my land.

All the other homeowners sold up quickly, wanting to get away before construction started, but I held on. I still had tenants paying rent, and the developers had investors clamouring about the delays. It took weeks of back and forth phone calls, but I finally settled for three times their value. They were just a bunch of old townhouses, ripe for renovation or demolition, in this case. And it was good business."

"So you'd advise me to sell Lorikeet Island?"

"Who to? Do you have a buyer lined up?"

Gaia chewed on the corner of her broken nail, one of yesterday's many casualties. "No. I don't think anyone would buy it right now. With the decline in the Chinese yuan and the plummeting iron ore prices, we've had to cut production everywhere else. We kept Lorikeet open, of course, but now…" She sighed. "I wish I was more like Mother, or that she was here. She'd know what to do."

"Maybe. Maybe not, too. Seems to me her bad decisions are what resulted in this mess. You need a different kind of thinking to get out of it. You might be exactly what the company needs." He tone softened. "You always had a plan, sweetheart, and I'm sure you have one now. Tell me – what do you intend to do?"

Gaia thought of the contract Jay had signed, sitting on her dining table. "I intend to rebuild. With the camp in ruins and the mine under water, that's a lot harder than I expected. We'll need alternate accommodation during construction. Something ready-made and nearby. Like the resort I'm staying at now." Jay's resort.

"Resorts aren't cheap," Chris said, "Especially if it's a luxury one. I saw one at a trade show this week asking a thousand dollars a night for one of the most basic rooms on the island, with the more upmarket accommodation at up to ten times that in peak season. Some gimmicky name, too – Romance or Valentine Island or something."

Gaia found herself nodding. "Yes, that's the one. Even with a substantial discount, their prices are much too high for staff, even in the short term. When iron ore prices were at their peak a few years ago, we might have considered it, but not now." She took a deep breath. "So I offered to buy the resort."

Chris laughed. "I bet that didn't go down well. That place was on the market a year ago – and it was overpriced then. The owners wouldn't want to sell at a loss."

"He didn't. When I explained to him that his property value would go down with the increased shipping traffic from the upgraded mine, and he'd be better off selling, he laughed. Like he didn't understand a thing about real estate."

Chris cleared his throat. "Hang on a second, sweetheart. You just handed him a negotiating tactic he could use against you. No wonder he laughed. Because if he blocks your upgrades by not helping you, you won't get him to cooperate at all. He's better off without the mine and he knows it, too. I thought the new owner would have to have more money than sense to buy that overpriced white elephant of a resort, but he sounds more shrewd than I gave him credit for. Who is he?"

"Jay Felix." Even as his name left her lips, Gaia's tummy flipped.

Chris swore. "The rock star? If I didn't know him, I'd definitely have said he had more money than sense. The guy's loaded, with fans buying everything he puts out. And he's got a real estate profile that rivals mine, because that's where he puts all his money. He beat me to a Melbourne property I had my eye on, too. Or at least, his investment advisers did. He might be a prize peacock, but whoever handles his investments doesn't play around. They won't let him sign a deal that doesn't bring him a hefty return."

Dread curled its tendrils down her throat. The contract he'd signed last night. Was it the same one her legal team had drawn up, or something else? Was that why he'd signed it so easily? She crossed to the table and flipped feverishly through the pages. No, it looked exactly like the one she'd printed. None of this made any sense. Maybe he really had been drunk last night. Drunk enough to sign away the resort he loved.

Could she truly take this place away from him?

"Daddy, what if I changed my mind, and decided not to buy the resort after all?"

"Then I think you'd be making a wise decision. If you get into a financial fight with that man, you won't win." Chris sucked in a breath. "Why would you change your mind, though? Last time I checked, you were as stubborn as Morrie. More so, maybe. When you have a plan, you see it through to the bitter end."

Gaia swallowed. "What if I don't want it to end...or be bitter?"

He laughed. "Now you sound like Morrie when I first met her. She wanted my client's property, and he didn't want to sell. We met for drinks, and one thing led to another and..." Chris coughed. "In the end, I did negotiate the agreement between them. She got what she wanted, and

I got the biggest commission I'd ever seen for closing the deal. I still think she did it out of love for me, though she denied it."

"Why didn't you and Mother stay together?" Gaia asked.

Chris sighed. "We separated for you, but I think it was just an excuse, really. I know your mother loved me as much as I loved her, but to her, that was unforgivable weakness. Something that made her softer than the hard persona she portrayed to everyone else, even you. I challenged her, made her feel less in control than she wanted to be. Something she just couldn't handle. So she lied to me, said she no longer loved me, and made me leave. I was her one weakness, and she was the love of my life."

"So you're saying…in order to be the chairman Mother was, I shouldn't fall in love? Because it's a weakness?" Gaia's heart sank. Her mother had said such things many times, but to hear it from her father, too…

"God, no! That was nearly thirty years ago. Morrie was a woman trying to make her way in what was predominantly a man's world, when most women her age were getting married, having children and staying home with them. She'd been brought up to believe in that. Most big Australian companies didn't have a single female senior executive, let alone chairman, back then. So she was fighting every day of her life, proving to herself and the men she worked with that she didn't belong at home with her children, when I think that's what she secretly wanted."

Gaia found that hard to believe. "Mother didn't like me. She avoided me as much as she could. Other kids got to play, but I had private tutors before and after school to make sure I was the best. On the rare occasions she was home, she was always working. If I interrupted her, I'd be sure of a lecture on everything she was doing and why. The school holidays were even worse, when she made me spend time in her office under the beady eyes of her nerdy assistants. She only stopped after I told her one had tried to kiss me when I was fifteen. Then she made me sit in on all her meetings. Ugh."

"Training you in business, I understand, but she didn't do any of that because she didn't like you. She avoided you because you were even more of a weakness for her than me." He coughed. "I'm sorry if your childhood was unhappy because of it. I shouldn't have given in to her, but it's too late for regrets now. I wanted to make her happy, but she wouldn't let me. Don't live a life as miserable as your mother's, sweetheart. No company is worth giving up everything – love, happiness and family – for. Promise me if you fall in love, you'll let yourself be happy."

"What if…what if I've already found someone?" Gaia's voice was so soft she could barely hear herself.

Chris evidently heard them loud and clear. "Already? Who's the lucky man?"

"Jay Felix. The owner of the resort." Gaia held her breath, but he didn't laugh, so she continued, "Ever since I met him, I get these feelings that I've never experienced with anyone else. My heart beats faster. I can't seem to take my eyes off him, even when he's on the other side of the room. He's nothing like the men in the office, or anyone Mother allowed me to associate with. He's not boring. He's…vibrant. Like everything that was missing in my life. And…he cares about me, too. I know he does. But I'm so conflicted, Daddy. About the island. I know it's best for the business to close this deal, whatever it takes, but I don't want to. This is his home, and it's where he belongs. Much more than me. If I try to take his island from him, he'll hate me." A tear slipped down her cheek. "I don't know what to do, Daddy."

"Do you love him?"

"Yes." The word fell from her lips before she'd even thought about it, but Gaia knew it was the truth. She'd never loved anyone like this in her life.

"And if you had to choose between him and Vasse Prospecting, which would you pick?" Chris pressed.

Gaia hung her head. Last night she'd picked Vasse Prospecting, and she felt sick at the thought. "It's not that simple, Daddy. The company – "

"Has all the staff it needs, ably led by James Stewart. Even Morrie admitted it, and that was a big thing for her. Let him run the company, while you look to your own life." His tone softened. "You're the only daughter I have, sweetheart. And I don't want you living the rest of your life with a broken heart, like Morrie and me. You deserve better. We both worked hard to make sure you have a better life than either of us. One with some happiness."

She didn't know what to say. That wasn't the advice she'd expected at all. "You think I should give up Mother's job for some guy?"

"He sounds like he's more than just some guy to you, sweetheart. The company won't collapse because there isn't a Vasse pulling all the strings. Stewart won't let that happen. Let the man do his job while you live a little. You'll still be the chairman of the company. Just make it more of a ceremonial role. Like being the queen."

Queen of Lorikeet Island, while Jay was king of Romance Island. A perfect match.

"Thank you, Daddy."

She ended the call, but she didn't put her phone down. Instead, she replied to Stewart's email with three words:

Approval granted. Proceed.

She set the phone down on the table, her attention drawn to the papers beside it. The ones Jay never should have signed. They weren't legally binding unless her signature sat beside his, as the representative of Vasse Prospecting. All she had to do was sign…

Screw the paperwork. She wanted Jay.

She picked up the one with Jay's signature on it and tore it in two. Then she proceeded to shred each page until no piece was larger than a postage stamp. There was nothing left for her to sign. Jay's island was safe.

FORTY-SIX

Gaia wanted to run back to Jay's house and tell him the good news, but she remembered what he'd said earlier: not to come back until she'd read those books, and was ready to try something kinky.

Was there even a jar of Nutella or peanut butter on the island? Even if there was, she wouldn't have the faintest idea where one put it to arouse someone.

Gaia sighed. After all, she'd watched all those awful adult movies, and learned nothing. Surely just reading a romance book couldn't be too bad. It's not like anyone would notice while she stayed in the privacy of her villa.

She unwrapped the books again, this time pulling all three volumes out. The covers looked innocuous enough — a tie, a carnival mask and a key. Not a jar of spread in sight.

A flash of pink caught her eye and Gaia felt all the blood drain from her face. Handcuffs? There was a pair of handcuffs hidden in the wrapping paper. Pink fluffy handcuffs, but handcuffs all the same. A gift from Jay, who apparently liked the things.

What part of being trussed up like a common criminal could possibly be sexy?

If she wanted to understand, evidently she had to read the books. Educational, he'd called them.

Grabbing what appeared to be the first volume, Gaia settled on the couch to learn.

FORTY-SEVEN

As a twenty-seven-year-old billionaire herself, Gaia was initially drawn to the man of Anastasia's dreams, secretly pleased that Jay had instantly made the comparison between her and the successful, male CEO. She even found herself grinning as the girl was whisked away in the billionaire's helicopter, much as she'd done to Jay.

But the more she read, the more she found herself siding with the girl and not the man at all. Jay had been the one to assist her when she was drunk, rescuing her from her distress more than once. That night with him had been the most incredible of her life, even if she didn't remember much of it.

The first sex scene took her breath away. After all, it was the first sex scene she'd ever read.

It was certainly a far cry from that romance book one of the girls had filched from her mother's nightstand. Full of men with throbbing swords that they thrust into quivering sheaths and other such nonsense. Helen had read it aloud as they whispered and giggled, until the book had been confiscated. It had certainly given her unreasonable expectations.

Gaia had been most disappointed when the first penis she saw had looked more like a cocktail sausage than a sword. Of course, it had certainly felt sharp enough when he'd jabbed it inside her on the fifth or sixth clumsy try. Three strokes and the deed was done; she'd given her virginity to Richard in the back of his BMW in the car park of the exclusive, all-boys college he attended, after the Year 12 ball. His school and hers had merged for the ball, and for a few minutes, so had they, before he'd sent the used condom sailing out the window into the night. Revolted by the whole experience, she'd pulled her knickers up and insisted he drive her home, where she'd spent an hour in the shower, scrubbing away the feel of his touch. She hadn't seen him again; she certainly hadn't wanted more sex from the boy.

Could a girl's first time really be as good as the one in the book? Gaia's certainly hadn't been. In fact, she'd never enjoyed herself for more than five minutes with a man before she'd spent the night with Jay. Did Jay have some secret superpower that allowed him to give pleasure for hours, or had she simply never met a man who knew what he was doing until Jay?

The billionaire in this book certainly knew what he wanted, and how to give and receive pleasure. He had the girl biting her lip, clenching her core and drooling over every inch of him even before he got undressed. Just like

Jay…

For the first time, she wondered if oral sex really was as awful as it looked in adult films. The book made it sound desirable, like sucking on a popsicle…

And if Jay did it to her…

Idly, she wondered if Jay owned a tie. Not necessarily one like on the cover of the book, but something tie-shaped that he could maybe tie her wrists with, to see if she liked it.

No, he probably didn't. She was surprised the man owned shoes.

Sighing, she read on.

Reading the contract made her squirm as it reminded her of her own preoccupation with paperwork. The girl agonised over the agreement she wanted to make with her billionaire almost as much as Gaia had over the one that was now confetti on her floor.

The next sex scene took her by surprise, almost as much as the heroine, it seemed, who hadn't been expecting to bring her billionaire to her bedroom. He became coarse and overbearing, but she liked it. Gaia squirmed again as she thought of Jay.

What if he were to tie her up, blindfold her, and do all sorts of sexy things to her? Would she refuse him? Her breath hitched.

Biting her lip, Gaia flipped back a few pages and read the sex scene again. No one had ever been that masterful with her in the bedroom. It was hot enough to make her insides melt.

Not for the first time, she thought of that time he'd slapped her bottom. How much she'd ached for sex to follow, but it hadn't. He'd barely touched her since. Well, not in an erotic way, anyway. Carrying her home didn't really count.

Feverishly, she kept reading, hoping for more sex. None of the business books had ever held her attention quite so completely.

Oh yes! She devoured every detail, wishing Jay were here so he could do all the things in the book. Gaia blushed. Letting a man have her at his mercy – tie her up! – wasn't her sort of thing at all. She'd spent a lifetime learning to dominate men, not the other way around. But maybe with Jay, it would be different…she could try it just the once and see if she liked it…

Satisfied, she returned to her book.

Wait…did he just say he was going to spank her? Like an unruly child from last century?

She reread the passage. Yes, he had. He wouldn't, though, surely. That was so degrading. Hardly romantic enough to go into a book.

And yet…he did. He was a man of his word, after all. Like Jay.

He'd turned the girl over his knee, pulled down her pants and spanked her. It had turned her on so much that they'd had explosive sex afterwards, better than before.

Gaia read the passage again, and again, her insides heating and clenching until her toes curled.

She imagined what it would feel like if Jay slapped her bottom again, like he had that night. He'd sent a zinging lightning bolt straight to her core then. What if he did it over and over and over until…until she was so aroused, she begged him to have sex with her? And he did?

Somehow, her knickers had become soaked while she

read. Had she spilled some water on herself somehow? She knew she couldn't have wet herself. Perhaps it was just hot in here and the perspiration had caused her clothes to stick to her. Yes. Of course. She wasn't used to tropical heat.

Gaia carefully earmarked the pages where the sex scenes started, including a particularly deep fold where the spanking took place, before she lost herself in the story again.

She didn't stop reading until she'd finished the book, when she went back and read all the erotic moments all over again.

Sometime in the early hours of the morning, she fell asleep, still clutching the well-thumbed paperback to her chest. Her dreams were things of delight, imagining every moment she'd read about, but not with some hero who only lived between the pages of a book. No, the man awakening every one of her senses and making her beg for more was Jay, the living, breathing hero who held her heart.

Jay was right. Being a billionaire was boring. What she wanted was to be someone's submissive, to learn the sublime bliss of losing control to him.

FORTY-EIGHT

The sun was high in the sky when the irritating chime of Gaia's phone forced her out of sleep. She ached more than ever, for needs unfulfilled. If only the dreams had been real.

She crawled out of bed and answered her phone.

"Miss Vasse?" Stewart asked.

Who else would answer her phone? "Yes?"

"Did you get my email?"

Gaia felt a dull sense of déjà vu. "About the layoffs? Yes. I sent you my response."

"No, the one I sent yesterday. About the future plans for Lorikeet Island, and the agreement with Romance Island Resort."

The resort? What? But she'd ripped up the contract. The pieces were still on the floor where she'd left them.

"I'm impressed. This sort of partnership isn't the way Vasse Prospecting has done business in the past, but

Morrigan refused to discuss joint ventures, no matter how lucrative. She would have simply bought the resort and run it into the ground, like she did with everything else on Lorikeet. I kept telling her we needed to build more relationships with the other businesses in the regions, but she always wanted to keep things within the Vasse family, she said. I didn't realise that you'd settled so well into the chairman position that you were considering taking the company in a completely new direction. I wish you'd discussed it with me first."

None of this made sense. "Stewart, I just woke up. What are you talking about?"

"I've spent the last week in negotiations with the owner of the resort and her manager. The turning point came yesterday when the cruise ship *True South* accepted our offer to relocate from Karratha to Lorikeet. She'll moor in the sound in about six weeks, which is the time it'll take to get a salvage crew together, anyway. Reconstruction will start in eight weeks, and it should be complete by the end of the dry season. Insurance will cover the construction costs, so it's not a huge issue if we need to extend the timeline into next year. But what they won't cover is the cost of flying in personnel by helicopter every day, which was our only option until the resort stepped in. This year, they'll be running a shuttle service from the mainland to the island for day trippers, with some cruises around the archipelago. Under our new agreement, those cruises will stop at the resort, Lorikeet Island and *True South*, so we'll be able to fly each shift of staff to the air strip at the pearl farm before ferrying them to Lorikeet. We'll be back in production in a matter of months; much earlier than I'd ever believed possible. The resort's also offered an employee discount to our staff when they book day trips or longer stays with them – sort of an employee incentive, but one we won't have to pay for. We'll resupply with the same boats as the resort uses until the Lorikeet airstrip is usable again, and – "

This was all new to Gaia. Jay hadn't mentioned a thing about day trips or *True South* or talking to Stewart, yet they'd been talking behind her back for a week? "Who told you all this?"

Stewart laughed. "As if you didn't know. This is all your doing, even if you left the details to Xan and me. Joanne said you and her brother cooked this up. And here I thought you were just having a holiday, and some sort of holiday fling. Xan and Joanne set me straight."

Names that meant nothing to Gaia. Oh, perhaps Xan…she was the hotel manager, wasn't she? But Gaia couldn't recall a Joanne. Wait, brother…did Jay have a sister? Surely he'd mentioned her once or twice. Something about slapping and helicopters? The corresponding flashback Gaia's mind brought up involved slapping, but the only woman in her dream had been herself, not someone else's sister. Incest. Ugh.

"I'm surprised you had time, what with your engagement and all. It's been all over the gossip magazines," Stewart finished.

Ah, yes. That. Gaia coughed, glad the voice-only call hid her flushed cheeks. Leaking the news about a fake engagement had been Stephanie's idea. Coupled with the photos, she was sure it would qualify as a cover story, and she'd been right. Now, she wished more than ever that the story was true.

"Anyway, I don't want to keep you. I just wanted to let you know that we've finalised the details, and the whole agreement's in your inbox, when you have time to read it. I'd say you've more than earned a holiday for the rest of your time up north. Pass on my thanks and congratulations to your fiancé, too."

Gaia mumbled a reply and ended the call.

Next, she called Jay. He answered on the fourth ring.

"Is it true that you sent your hotel manager to my company to negotiate an agreement behind my back?" Gaia demanded, striving to sound like her usual imperious self.

Jay exhaled noisily into the phone receiver. "I wouldn't say behind your back. I told you I let my people sort this sort of stuff out for me, and you said you did the same. Jo and Xan knew what they were doing. I sent them a copy of that first contract and they took it from there."

"But…you signed the first contract. Why would you do that if you knew they were negotiating a new one?"

"You were really, really upset and I asked if I could do anything to help. You said you'd feel better if I signed, so I did. End of story."

Gaia still didn't get it. "But why would you sign away your resort just to make me feel better?"

Jay laughed. "I didn't sign away the resort, baby. I just autographed a contract. If you wanted it to be legally binding, you need signatures from both the owners, or one and a delegate. Without two signatures, you don't have a deal. Whatever Jo and Xan signed in Perth, now that's legally binding. But they know what they're doing. Me? I'm just the rock star hotel owner who put up most of the money for the place. They look after the business side of it."

"Why didn't you tell me?" she persisted.

"Talk business when you're supposed to be enjoying your holiday? Baby, you should know the last thing I ever want to talk about is business. Jo and Xan keep me up to date with what I need to know. Not my fault your people don't let you into the loop. Maybe they wanted you to enjoy your holiday, too." He made the whole thing sound like nothing, when it meant everything to her.

Gaia barely noticed when the call ended, she was so preoccupied with her own thoughts.

How could she ever thank him, let alone repay him? He'd done so much for her, and not because he wanted a reward. She had nothing he needed, while he was everything she wanted. A man who cared about her, who'd do whatever it took to make her happy.

He'd even sent her the books in an effort to make her sex life less boring. Maybe he did want something from her after all. The question was, was she willing to give it to him? It's not like spending the night with him would be some sort of sacrifice. No, it was pleasure beyond her wildest dreams, or it had been so far.

She sat back and stared at her phone. Somehow, Jay had saved Lorikeet Island, all while he was enjoying himself up here with her. He'd sent two women to negotiate with Stewart on his behalf. Trusted them to do what was best for his business, so he could make the most of his wealth.

Gaia wanted that. Badly. Was it really as simple as Daddy had said? Could she trust Stewart with Vasse Prospecting while she fulfilled her sexual fantasies with Jay?

Gaia giggled. She wasn't even sure if they could be

anything more than fantasies yet. What if she didn't like being spanked?

There was only one way to find out. Was she ready?

FORTY-NINE

Not really. For a start, she didn't have so much as a condom in the house, let alone any of the other items she longed to try out. The maid had said something about a room service menu, though…

Gaia grabbed the menu off the kitchen counter, but all she found was a list of food and drinks. Not even a jar of peanut butter.

No, wait. She'd said it was in the bedroom. Gaia pulled open the drawers until she found a red folder. Inside, the first page proclaimed that it was the Red Book of Pleasure, supplying all her romance needs. Feeling her face grow hot, Gaia turned the page.

She almost dropped it when she saw the picture of what could only be a vibrator. When she could bring herself to look at it again to read the description, the headline said it all: THE SELF-LOVE PACKAGE.

Dreading what she'd find next, Gaia steeled herself, but the next product turned out to be some sort of basic honeymoon package, containing an assortment of condoms, lubricants and massage oils. That didn't sound so bad. A deluxe version included a selection of sex toys, plus instructions on how to use them.

There were costumes, for one or both partners, that left Gaia shaking her head. Snow White and Red Riding Hood were children's stories, not the sort of thing that should be associated with sex, surely. And the adult-sized baby costume? Ugh. The more she saw, the more she wanted to put the book down and give up on the whole crazy idea. But some nagging voice inside her drove her on. She reached the final page of the book, which was a double page spread under the headline FIFTY SHADES OF ROMANCE. There was a blindfold, a tie, a riding crop, baby oil…Gaia didn't need to read any more. She called room service and placed her order.

Then she lay on the bed, already feeling spent.

What would it feel like to have her wrists tied to the bedhead?

She lifted her head to look, only to find that the bedhead was made of a solid piece of timber, with nothing to tie anything onto.

Her dream died.

It was a stupid dream, anyway, Gaia decided, striding out of the villa. She'd work off her frustration with a brisk walk along the beach.

FIFTY

The tide was out and Gaia intended to walk the length of her private beach until she calmed down, but she stopped when she realised the beach wasn't at all private today. Two workmen were busily assembling a structure in the sand, where the tide didn't quite reach.

"Afternoon, ma'am," one said.

Torn between wanting to tell him to go away or demand what he was doing on her private beach, instead, Gaia said, "What is it?"

"It's a daybed, ma'am. A sort of sunlounge for two. The hotel manager wants them installed before she flies back tomorrow. This is the last one left to do. If you want to see what it'll look like when it's finished, there's one over at Villa Pinctada, next door."

Gaia headed back the way she'd come, then rounded the screening vegetation to the private beach next to hers. Sure enough, the man was right – there was a metal frame like the one she'd seen on her beach, only this one was more than just a few struts. The beams formed a sort of four-poster bed, with opaque roller blinds on the three sides that didn't face the ocean. A canopy kept the sun and rain off the mattress and scattered cushions beneath. With a bed like this, she wouldn't need a bedhead. Jay could tie her hands to one of the corner posts. Pulling down the blinds would give them complete privacy, in which he could do whatever he wanted to her.

Now all she had to do was wait until the workmen were finished with her private playground. She marched back to her villa and sat on the veranda, where she could watch the men at work. They were constructing her fantasy, after all. She couldn't wait to tell Jay.

FIFTY-ONE

"Meet me at my private beach in an hour," Gaia told Jay, her voice breathless with excitement. Her mood wavered between thrilled and terrified. Thrilled at the thought of what Jay would do to her, and terrified of what she might feel. The room service basket had arrived, but the wave of panic that had washed over her at the sight of so many things she had no idea what to do with made her set it aside without opening it. Once she'd experimented a little with Jay on the beach, if she liked it, she'd bring him back here to play some more. "I've arranged a surprise to thank you for everything you've done."

"Will there be handcuffs? There better be handcuffs, baby, because if this is another get drunk, lie back and be boring seduction like the last few times, you can just say thank you over the phone now and I'm good," Jay drawled.

"It'll be different. I promise." She hung up before she

spoiled the surprise and told him what she had planned.

Handcuffs. She had to find the fluffy ones he'd given her.

The maid had come to tidy the place already, so the ripped up contract and the wrapping paper had vanished, too. Gaia prayed she hadn't thrown out the handcuffs along with the wrapping as she desperately searched the house. If she couldn't find them, she'd need to ring room service again to get a replacement. Trying not to blush when the first order had arrived had been hard enough, but to have to face the waiter again for another one...Gaia shuddered.

But the cuffs were nowhere to be found. Not on the dining table, and not on the floor. Had the maid taken them for herself?

Maybe she would be better off buying a new pair from room service. At least they'd be clean.

Gaia surrendered and opened the drawer containing the Red Book. Resting on top of it were the pink cuffs. She almost cried in relief.

Next, she had to choose the right clothes. Of course, she intended to remove them as soon as possible, but she had no intention of showing up that way. Imagine walking around the resort naked! Not even Jay would be daring enough to do such a thing.

Something easy to remove, she decided. Anything from the resort collection would do, but she wanted something a little bit sexy, too. Not too revealing. Something...demure. Gaia settled for a halter-neck dress, tying the straps in a bow at the nape of her neck. There. She was properly gift-wrapped.

On her way out, she grabbed the ice bucket full of

supplies for the evening. Enough to do them for an hour or two before returning to her villa for more.

The sand was soft beneath her sandalled feet, dried to powder in the afternoon sun as it waited for the tide to come back to caress it. She knew exactly how it felt.

Her sunbed was waiting for her, now as complete as the one next door, with cream and grey cushions piled on the grey mattress. Gaia set the ice bucket on a shelf that seemed made for it; perhaps it was. She let down the blinds, which billowed a little in the breeze. A quick check reassured her that the filmy fabric hid the bed from sight. The only way to see in was to stand directly in front, between the bed and the ocean. Jay wouldn't see what awaited him until he was almost close enough to touch.

The scrunch of footsteps on the sand made her check her watch. Her hour was almost up, and Jay was on time for once. Her heart beat frantically in her chest. Could she do this?

Maybe if she had a drink to settle her nerves…

She poured champagne into two glasses, downing the contents of one before refilling it.

Gaia reached for the handcuffs and fastened them around her left wrist. Burying her restrained hand amid the cushions, she struck a pose on the edge of the bed, with her legs crossed and peeping out from the end. She reached for the glass, holding it in her free hand as she waited for Jay.

She didn't have to wait long. Before she could even see him, he called, "Someone said something about handcuffs."

"I did, yes. Wine?" she offered, holding out her glass.

Jay stepped into view. Wearing nothing but a pair of low-slung shorts, he looked as succulent as the moment she first met him. Everything she'd ever wanted.

"Yours is over there." She pointed at a glass on the ledge near the head of the bed, which he'd have to crawl across the mattress to reach.

He didn't move. "You going to get it for me? You're closer."

Gaia felt an unfamiliar urge to obey, just like the girl in the book. But that wasn't part of her plan. Under cover of the cushions, she snaked the cuffs around one of the bed posts, then clipped the other cuff around her right wrist. She lifted her restrained wrists, the chain tinkling against the bedpost. "I can't. I'm a little tied up right now."

Jay grinned. "Like that, is it? This'll be interesting." He bounced onto the bed beside her and scrambled up to grab his glass.

Gaia hadn't thought this through properly. Drinking her champagne while wearing handcuffs was a lot harder than she thought it would be. When she finally managed to bring her lips to the glass, she drained it, then threw it on the sand. The bubbles burned in her blood, making her lightheaded as she moved onto her hands and knees, facing away from Jay.

"Those look new." His fingers slid beneath the waistband of her knickers and pinged the elastic against her hip. Pleasure zinged straight to Gaia's core at the sting.

Now she was glad she'd worn the skimpy underwear, though she'd never liked g-strings before. "I wore them for you. I know what I want now."

"Really?" She heard him sip his champagne. "Enlighten me."

"I want you – "

He snorted. "I could have guessed that for myself."

Gaia bit her lip. "I want you to spank me. I've been a bad girl."

"Oh yeah?"

"And then I want you to – " She swallowed, struggling to spit out the coarse words, but somehow she managed: " – fuck me hard."

His hand stroked her bottom. "You don't sound so sure."

"I am! I've never wanted anything more than I want this now!" she insisted. Was the man going to make her beg?

The hand stopped stroking. "So you do this a lot, then?"

Gaia swallowed. "No. This will be my first time. Go gently with me, please?"

Silence, then his voice came out low and angry. "So you think I make it a habit of hitting women, and having rough sex with them? Have you got Shou hiding in the bushes taking pictures again? Did he tell you I like hurting women?"

Gaia sagged. "No. I haven't seen the pilot since we flew with him out to the falls together. It's just us out here. You and me. I…want you, Jay. I want you to do all the things the billionaire does in the books you gave me. Only…while I'm in bed with you, I don't want to be the billionaire." There. She'd admitted it.

"So you want me to rip your clothes off?"

Her breathing hitched. "Yes."

He undid the dress, so the front fell away, baring her breasts. He yanked it over her hips and dragged it down her legs, then threw it onto the sand. "These should go, too." He seized the elastic at her waist and pulled until it snapped, the broken end whipping her across the butt cheek.

"Ow!" she yelped, clenching her thighs together as the sting sparked something in her core.

"I thought you liked pain."

"I don't know," she lied. "This is all new to me." She wanted to beg and scream for more, but she bit her lip to stop herself. He had her naked and at his mercy, handcuffed to the bed. "Do whatever you want to me. Just…be gentle."

"Spank you, fuck you hard, but be gentle. Baby, do you have any idea what you want? Or is this just a show for more material you can sell to the press about me?"

Press? What press?

"You'll be naked in the pictures, you know. Not the image of the billionaire businesswoman at all. Is that what you want? Naked pictures of you plastered all over the internet? I mean, I know there's plenty of me around. I don't mind. But the media isn't as forgiving when it's a woman."

Desperation turned her voice into a squeak. "There isn't anyone else here but us, I swear! I know I've been a bad girl. With the photographs and the press and your island and everything. Spank me. Punish me. Do whatever you want to me, please. I want you, Jay. I want you!"

"Will you still want me if I suggest we go back to my place, where I know there aren't any cameras? Or if I say no to spanking you, because it's not my thing?" Feather-light fingers caressed her bottom again.

"Yes. Anything you want. Yes!"

Jay cleared his throat. "Well, then. We better get you out of those cuffs, because we're not taking the bed with us.

Where are the keys?"

The blood drained from Gaia's face. "Keys?" she choked out.

Jay laughed. "You mean you just handcuffed yourself to a bed but you didn't think to bring keys? Baby, you're crazier than I thought. I don't suppose you learned how to pick handcuffs in that snobby private school you went to?"

Gaia shook her head.

"I could call one of the guys from Maintenance. They'd be delighted to help. Might take a while, though. Hours, maybe."

Gaia shrank inside. Let strange men see her like this? She'd rather die. "We could do things while we wait."

"What, play strip poker? You don't have a stake left, baby. Besides, I already told you. Sadism isn't really my thing." Jay's tone turned thoughtful. "You know, if you stood on the bed, we might be able to pull them right over the top of the bedposts. It looks like there's a gap in the frame up there that's big enough."

With Jay's help, she scrambled to her feet, stretching her arms up until they almost reached the top of the bedpost. She couldn't see over the frame, but Jay assured her the gap was there.

He peered at something over her head for a few seconds before he said, "I think if you jump, you should be able to get up high enough. Just watch your head and aim for the sand." His arms stayed around her, though, wrapping her naked body in an embrace she didn't want to end. Then it did, as he stepped away from the bed. "Right, on three, baby. One, two…"

"Three!" Gaia leaped, but something held her back, so

even as she flew toward the sand, she swung back toward the bed. Her body slammed against the bedpost, knocking the breath from her lungs. But she didn't fall, like she expected to. Instead, she dangled from her wrists, caught in the cuffs that had somehow gotten stuck in the frame. Gaia scrambled for a foothold to take her weight off her aching wrists, but she could only touch the bed with two toes. Nowhere near enough to make a difference. "Help me!" she pleaded.

Jay bounced onto the bed. A moment later, she cried out in pain as the cuffs yanked her wrists. "You're stuck up here, baby. The chain's caught on a bolt on the frame. You're going to be hanging out here for a while. I'll have to call Maintenance now."

"Please," she begged. "My arms hurt. Help me…take my weight. Please."

"Oh. Right." Jay jumped onto the sand, staring at her for a moment before he stepped closer. "Wrap your legs around me. That should help."

Gaia spun helplessly as she tried to do what he'd asked, until he seized her hips and guided her legs into place. She tightened her hold and the pressure on her arms eased. She breathed a sigh of relief and kissed him.

Jay seemed surprised for a moment, before he returned her kiss, his tongue teasing hers to come out and play. Gaia gladly obeyed, pouring all her desire into her kiss. No, not hers any more, but his. Just like the rest of her body. Her breasts softened against his chest, her toes curled against his bottom and it felt like Mitchell Falls were pooling in her belly, aching to stroke the hardening, growing ridge at the juncture of her thighs.

But the ridge wasn't part of her. It was all… "Jay," she gasped. She squirmed against him, all hot and hard and a million times yes. "I want you. I need you."

"Yeah, I sort of guessed that, what with the way you're soaking through my shorts and all." His eyes seemed to bore into her, melting everything in their path on the way to her soul. "You know, pain might not be my thing, but this is my kind of kink. A pair of handcuffs, a crazy position to try and a girl who's close to losing control. I think I can tip you over that edge, baby. Would you like to fly with me?"

She needed to feel him inside her. Now. "Yes, please. Anything. I'm yours, Jay."

"Loosen your legs, baby," he instructed, seizing her thighs. She did as she was bid, before he hoisted her up higher as he stepped back.

"What are you – " she began, her body swinging out over the sand.

"Trust me, baby." He settled her legs over his shoulders. Gaia's heart stuttered as she realised he had his head between her legs. Not just his head. His hot tongue slipped inside her and she almost exploded on the spot. Exploded in the air, suspended between the bed she'd handcuffed herself to and the man she wanted more than anything.

Gaia moaned, writhing as he pleasured her with his mouth while she was helpless to stop him. She didn't want him to stop. Damn, she wanted him to do this to her forever.

If this was what oral sex felt like, she didn't want to see another penis for the rest of her life. It was –

Boom. The explosion inside her was bigger than any controlled detonation at a minesite. Jay had laid enough delectable dynamite to blow her to pieces with just his tongue.

"Baby, you're so wet, I could drink from your pussy," Gaia heard Jay say from far away. She felt him move beneath her, walking while her legs were still slung over his shoulders, but she wasn't paying attention because the electrifying aftershocks from her orgasm still coursed through her.

Unbelievable. Indescribable. Incredible. Burning cold.

Gaia yelped as icy coldness engulfed her lady bits. She tried to twist away, but Jay held her firm.

"Hold still, baby. I want to see which tastes better – you or the wine."

Gaia watched in fascination as he poured more champagne inside her. This was sexier than anything in the book.

"Would you like a taste, baby?" He didn't wait for her to reply. Instead, he tipped the bottle up to her lips and poured. Champagne trickled into her mouth, but it also ran down her chin, creating a cascade down her breasts in all directions. He poured until the last drops touched her tongue, then he threw the bottle on the sand. Without warning, he turned his own tongue on her super-sensitive lady bits.

She moaned louder this time, and not just once, either. Every moment she begged him for more pleasure. Every stroke of his tongue sent shockwaves through her, her desire far more potent than the champagne bubbles bursting in her brain. She shrieked as she came a second time, barely feeling when he lifted her legs off his shoulders and drew them down to his hips again.

Panting, she slowly became aware of the hot, hard ridge between her thighs. Except…she couldn't feel the fabric of his shorts any more. Gaia glanced down at…well, she couldn't call that a cocktail sausage. The man had a monstrous penis, so big she was scared it wouldn't fit inside her. He'd already sheathed it in a condom, ready to go.

"But I wanted more orgasms like that last one," she pouted.

He leaned in, so his mouth was beside her ear, while that hard length pressed against her thigh. "Baby, that was just foreplay. What I can do with my mouth is nothing compared to what you'll feel when I'm buried deep inside you. It's ecstasy, heaven, nirvana and the best natural high you will ever have. And you will beg for more."

Gaia moistened her suddenly dry mouth. "Then fuck me. Please." She pressed against him, gasping as she felt him start to slide inside her. God, that felt good.

But he didn't give her any more. Not yet. Instead, he walked her forward until her back was pressed against the bedpost, her arms straight up above her head. "So that's a yes?" he asked.

Gaia nodded, gasping as he filled her completely. He fit just fine. So fine… "Oh, yes, yes," she moaned, squirming.

Slowly, steadily, he moved, like he was being careful not to hurt her. "How does that feel, baby?"

"Faster," she begged. "Harder."

He mustn't have heard her. He slowed the pace even more, driving deep inside her before withdrawing almost completely.

Gaia wiggled, trying to hurry him up.

He pinned her hips to the bedpost, so she couldn't

move them, and withdrew. "Who's in control here?" he demanded, his hands curling around her bottom.

"You are," she said, sighing in bliss as he filled her again.

"So I get to call the pace. Unless you want to stop, of course. If you don't want this, just say so."

Another toe-curling thrust took her breath away, so it was several seconds before she could gasp out, "Don't stop. Never stop. Oh my God, I love you, Jay." As the sensations built inside her, her words slipped into incoherent moaning, pounded into dust by his relentless pace until he sent her soaring with another screaming orgasm.

She became aware of Jay swearing, growling something she couldn't understand, until he stilled inside her, his eyes turned heavenward. Gaia smiled. She'd made it as good for him as he had for her.

"Baby, are those my handcuffs? The ones I gave you?"

His calm words startled her. She glanced up. "Yes." She hadn't been able to bring herself to open any of the items in the kinky gift basket, so this was all she had.

"Those don't need keys." He reached up and clicked one cuff, then the other. Carefully, he helped her lower her arms to her chest.

Still quivering from her massive release, not to mention still impaled by the man who'd given it to her, Gaia wasn't sure whether to be angry or relieved. "Did you do that on purpose? Leave me dangling there so long so I'd have sex with you?"

Jay laughed. "Baby, you were begging for it on the bed, remember? I was the one who wanted to go inside. Still do. The sun will go down soon, and the crabs will come out. Sex with crabs is not something I want to share with you."

Gaia shivered. "Did you do that on purpose?" she repeated.

Jay set her down on the sand, sliding out of her. "The incredible sex? Yes. Leave you in handcuffs? No. I forgot. I was kind of distracted." He gestured at her body. "Pretty naked girl, begging for sex and desperate for me. I couldn't refuse."

Gaia beamed. "You think I'm pretty?"

"Yeah. With your skin sticky with champagne, your just-fucked hair, your face flushed and your voice breathless from screaming my name through the best orgasms of your life…you look real pretty, Gaia." His sincere smile held no trace of laughter. He really meant it. "Now, on rare occasions, I have given into a pretty girl's desires and spanked her, but only in the privacy of my hotel room. So if you're serious about wanting to spend the evening with me, and maybe forgive me for forgetting things, would you like to come back to my place tonight?"

Gaia considered him. Who was she kidding? She couldn't say no to him. Not with the taste of him still on her lips. "Only if we bring the handcuffs with us. And stop off at my place for some toys I'd like to try."

Jay's eyes lit up. "Toys, hmm? How can I say no to that? You're on, baby."

On top, maybe, Gaia thought, then reconsidered. Anywhere Jay wanted her to be, really. Every atom in her body was irrevocably, unbelievably his. Just the way she wanted it to be.

FIFTY-TWO

Gaia climbed stiffly into the helicopter, wincing as the seat cushioning wasn't quite soft enough beneath her tender behind. Maybe she shouldn't have told Jay about how she'd set the media on his little tart. She considered, then shook her head. She didn't regret it for a moment. Jay's anger had turned his soft pats into stinging slaps that turned her on so much she wanted him to spank her all over again this morning. Now it would be a week before she could sit down without remembering the feeling of his hands on her. Good.

As the helicopter rose into the air, her gaze swept the island. Romance Island Resort, where she'd known more romance in one night than she'd seen in a lifetime before it. And she still had two books to read, to inspire her to greater, more pleasurable heights she'd never believed possible. All because of Jay Felix, a man like no other. She might be leaving him now, but she'd be back. Nothing would keep her from Jay for long.

224

The story continues in
The Rock Star Wants A Wife

ABOUT THE AUTHOR

Demelza Carlton has always loved the ocean, but on her first snorkelling trip she found she was afraid of fish.

She has since swum with sea lions, sharks and sea cucumbers and stood on spray drenched cliffs over a seething sea as a seven-metre cyclonic swell surged in, shattering a shipwreck below.

Demelza now lives in Perth, Western Australia, the shark attack capital of the world.

The *Ocean's Gift* series was her first foray into fiction, followed by her suspense thriller *Nightmares* trilogy. She swears the *Mel Goes to Hell* series ambushed her on a crowded train and wouldn't leave her alone.

Want to know more? You can follow Demelza on Facebook, Twitter, YouTube or her website, Demelza Carlton's Place at:

www.demelzacarlton.com

Books by Demelza Carlton

Ocean's Gift series

Ocean's Gift (#1)
Ocean's Infiltrator (#2)
Ocean's Depths (#3)
Water and Fire

Turbulence and Triumph series

Ocean's Justice (#1)
Ocean's Trial (#2)
Ocean's Triumph (#3)
Ocean's Ride (#4)
Ocean's Cage (#5)
Ocean's Birth (#6)
How To Catch Crabs

Nightmares Trilogy

Nightmares of Caitlin Lockyer (#1)
Necessary Evil of Nathan Miller (#2)
Afterlife of Alana Miller (#3)

Romance Island Resort series

Maid for the Rock Star (#1)
The Rock Star's Email Order Bride (#2)
The Rock Star's Virginity (#3)
The Rock Star and the Billionaire (#4)
The Rock Star Wants A Wife (#5)
The Rock Star's Wedding (#6)

9 781925 799088